The Secret in the Dump

David Lewis

SCRIPTURE UNION
130 City Road, London EC1V 2NJ

First published 1983

ISBN 0 86201 184 1

Phototypeset by Wyvern Typesetting Limited, Bristol
Printed by Ebenezer Baylis & Son Limited,
The Trinity Press, Worcester, and London

1

Penny Bunn struggled and wrestled with the safety pin, her stomach and the top of her jeans. Two more tugs and a deep breath and she would get the tops of her jeans together. Penny's jeans never fitted her properly! If the front fitted, then the legs were miles too long. If the legs were the right length, the tops had to be hooked together with two-inch, extra-strong safety pins. Safety pins were Penny's best friends.

'There!' grunted Penny sucking in her rather large stomach. 'Done it!'

Penny slowly breathed out, making sure that no sudden tension was placed on the metal rods that held her together. Her ample folds ebbed, like waves over the sea until the extra-strong safety pin vanished under the crashing surf of her flesh! She took her chewing gum out of her mouth and stuck it behind her ear until after breakfast, during which time, if her mother wasn't looking, she would dunk it in the sugar bowl.

She opened her large, oak wardrobe that her parents had bought in the jumble sale for 50p and stared critically into the yellowing mirror.

'Mirror, mirror on the wall,
Who is the fattest girl of all?'
she whispered miserably. She turned sideways and saw that her stomach did stick out – a lot! Again, she sucked in her breath and that made a little difference.

Her lungs exploded with a gasping report and her front shot out again, placing sudden increased strain on the safety pin; but it held fast. 'No one,' she deduced, 'could walk around all day with their breath sucked in anyway.'

A sooty pigeon landed on her window-sill and confidently tapped the glass with its beak.

'Good morning, my angel,' cooed Penny, forgetting her besetting worry. 'Hang on, haven't made my bed yet!'

She threw back the blankets and neatly swept all the biscuit crumbs and broken crisps into one hand. Opening the window she carefully sprinkled them in front of the bird. 'You'll get fat, mind!' she admonished innocently.

Penny quickly tidied her bedroom by pushing everything higgledy-piggledy under the bed.

The smell of frying bacon drew her downstairs like a magnet attracting nails. Penny sat down in a daze listening to the sizzling and spluttering of her breakfast.

'Elbows off, dear,' muttered Mrs. Bunn without looking round. Penny didn't hear and made islands and rivers in her porridge. Then she bombed her islands with large dollops of syrup.

'Eat up, dear,' encouraged Mrs. Bunn, scratching at the frying pan. 'It's a lovely day and we don't want you fainting of hunger in the middle of playing, do we, dear?' Penny attacked the plate of bacon, eggs and fried bread. Mrs. Bunn, as large and jolly as Penny, always ended her sentences with 'dear'. Penny had grown not to mind, and anyway, it was better than 'darling'.

6

As breakfast proceeded Penny's safety pin bent a little. She thumped back upstairs to signal the gang. Today was the day when they were going to meet outside Webster's shop and then make their den in the Dump even more secret.

The pigeon had gone and so had the crumbs. Leaning out of the window, Penny grabbed hold of a piece of string which was tied to the drainpipe and gave it a mighty tug.

The string from Penny Bunn's house dangled and looped across two gardens and a back lane into Mrs. Hooper's garden, number 31 Balaclava Street, and ended tied to a dozen tin cans fixed to the pole of her washing line.

Owly Hooper sat on a lawn-mower box outside his back kitchen door. Three soot stained walls kept the Hoopers safe from dogs, gypsies, tramps and children; the latter being worse than all the others put together.

Owly was engaged in his daily repairs to his large, thick spectacles. On his knee he balanced sellotape, string, two bits of copper wire and a safety pin and paper clip. For a boy of ten years, who found even combing his thick black hair an effort, he could accomplish a remarkably good job. That is, if you didn't mind looking like a radio-active hedgehog afterwards! The trouble was, that when he took off his spectacles to repair them, he was as blind as a bat and could not *see* to do it. He fumbled through half closed eyes and a tangle of black hair. A big black and white cat stretched, sunning itself in an enormous rhubarb patch. Only rhubarb and gooseberries grew in their garden, and no one liked either; but then, nothing seemed to grow anywhere in this dingy part of London, only grass and weeds. This gave Owly the greatest relief because there was nothing to spoil in the garden! There were no flowers to crush or beans to knock over – he could play football, glorious football for ever, with no one to shout at him to be careful.

Owly squinted through his half closed eyes and then opened them as wide as possible. For some reason or other this made him see slightly better. He puffed and grunted when the sellotape stuck together and he had to start all over again. The pins and wire fell off his knee and the lawn-mower box began to hurt him. He shifted slightly and *everything* fell off. 'Blummy scum!' he exploded. Since he wasn't allowed to swear he had invented words to say in moments of urgency and exasperation. He dared anyone to tell him off, for these were his very own words, so they couldn't possibly be swear words!

Mrs. Hooper, her hair still in rollers, leaned around the kitchen door. 'What you going to do today, love?'

'Not much,' hissed Owly through the pins and wire held tightly between his teeth. 'S'pose I'll go down to Webster's and then we're going exploring in the Dump.'

'That'll be nice,' cooed Mrs. Hooper unthinkingly as she wheeled Cyril's pram into the summer stillness of the flowerless garden. Mrs. Hooper spoke to Owly but stared lovingly at the baby. 'Keep an eye on him, love. I'm just starting the washing up.' Owly grunted vaguely and carried on with his invention.

Cyril, aged eight months, blissfully asleep, drifted in a world of silence and calm. Under the gooseberry bushes two blackbirds unsuccessfully tried to scratch a hole through to Australia. Mrs. Hooper sang softly to herself in the kitchen, something about Yellow Submarines.

In the distance a Thames tug hooted like an owl lost from the night. Owly blew the hair out of his eyes, only for it to fall back again. Carefully he held a thin piece of wire directly above two lined up holes in his glasses and tried to thread it through.

Suddenly there was a clanging, banging, dashing, crashing sound. Owly stuck the wire into his finger and yelled. Rover, the cat, jumped a metre in the air, through a rhubarb leaf into the pram. Cyril screamed as only a baby disturbed in the land of Nod can scream and Mrs. Hooper dropped a best saucer, smash into the sink.

'Not again!' moaned Mrs. Hooper.

Now more composed Owly called, 'It's OK Mum. It's only our secret sign!'

Owly immediately pegged a home made skull and cross-bones flag on the washing line and hoisted it as high as it would go.

'I'm off, Mum – going to see Penny and Robin by Webster's.'

*   *   *

Mrs. Potts, Robin's mother, wasn't in rollers. She cleaned and polished her house in what she called 'sensible' clothes. As she dusted the coffee table near the double-glazed picture window she glanced down the neatly mowed lawn but what caught her eye was the skull and cross bones flying frantically on the Hoopers' washing line! Inwardly she groaned but without showing any signs of misgiving she called up stairs, 'Robin – that flag is flying again!'

High up in the attic Robin carefully washed his painting brush. It was a special one and had cost 80p and had a good sharp point. His bedroom, with its two new dormer windows in the roof, had only recently been made for him. The room had sloping walls, very much like a boat turned upside down. From the window where he sat he could see the river and the tugs nosing about on it like lazy water beetles. To the left he could see Owly's washing line and further away the gasworks.

All around the walls were posters and pictures of football teams and footballers. Robin loved football – but he wasn't allowed to play it.

'He's delicate, you know,' Mrs. Potts would often say to people. In order to keep him occupied she continually bought Robin plastic modelling kits. The sole idea was to keep him off the streets! Robin, poor boy, had dozens of them, ranging from Napoleonic soldiers to dinosaurs, British birds, aeroplanes and weird monsters. Boxes, piled high, just waited for him to catch up. He never did, due to the fact that a clutch of aunts and uncles and grandparents thought, on observing the pile of boxes that he *liked* making them! For everyone, birthday and Christmas presents were easy – always a plastic model.

Actually Robin didn't mind making them. It was the endless backlog that got him down. 'Back by lunch time,' called Robin kicking his football slyly out of the kitchen doorway. Mrs. Potts sighed worriedly but said nothing to stop him. She called after him, 'Have you got a vest on?' But Robin was gone.

2

Owly, Penny and Rip arrived at Webster's corner shop almost at the same time and sat on the edge of the pavement (Robin was called Rip by his friends because R.I.P. were his initials). The gutter was full of ice-cream papers, cigarette ends, Coke tins and bus tickets.

'How much money you got?' asked Penny. Rip as usual was the only one with any money and he tipped his pocket out on to the pavement. Owly slapped one coin down flat before it rolled down the drain. '22p, and that's all until Friday,' moaned Rip.

'Come on,' grinned Owly, 'let's spend it all and take the stuff down the Dump!'

Webster's shop window was a dead window. Everything in it, from boxes of chocolates to cigarettes was artificial. The dust of years had settled on every plastic chocolate and banana. It wasn't a shop in the supermarket sense. Mrs. Webster had opened the shop in her front room when her husband had been killed years ago. 'Squashed he was, poor man,' Mr. Sharoom had said, recounting the unhappy event to the police. 'Saw it myself – squashed between a cargo boat and the harbour wall.' Then leaning on his road sweeper's brush added with gusto, 'Flat as a jam pancake he was!'

Under the hot sun, the plastic bananas in the window had softened and hung like sad, anaemic yellow stalactites from the hooks. Prepared though they were, when the children pushed open the inside door and the door bell clanged, they jumped, startled by the sudden sharpness of the sound. Penny whispered in the darkness (you always whispered in Webster's), 'Where is she?'

Nothing was touchable in the whole of the shop. Between the customers and Mrs. Webster there had been erected a chicken wire fence. No one was going to steal in that shop! Though it had been known for little fingers to worm their way through the holes in the wire mesh and hook out a jelly baby or packet of chewing gum. Behind the dimly-lit counter, dusty shelves reached up to the black ceiling. On the top shelf there were jars and boxes containing sweets and toffees, long since all stuck together, forming large, jar-shaped lollipops of toffee or boiled sweets. No one bought anything off the top shelf! Lower down, however, were more fresh things but Mrs. Webster, with an eye to children's teeth, also sold scrubbed and cleaned carrots, which floated like goldfish in a bowl of water on the counter. Strangely enough they sold reasonably well, which pleased Mrs. Webster, parents, and, no doubt, the purchasers as well. On Fridays there were toffee apples, and on Friday nights toothache by the street-full. It happened every week.

They hardly heard Mrs. Webster shuffle into the shop in her bedroom slippers. It wasn't that the poor lady was sinister or that she hated children, it was just the way she looked at you over her steel-rimmed glasses, and the way that some children teased her and muttered rude things about her ginger wig!

'What do you want?' she coughed.

Rip slapped all the money on the counter. 'That much worth of liquorice allsorts please.'

Not ruffled by the strange order, Mrs. Webster carefully weighed out the appropriate amount on the brass scales. 'Could you put some of the coconut ones in too, please?' added Owly. This she did but puffed and blew as if it was a great deal of trouble. 'Don't slam the door, please!' added Mrs. Webster and put her hands over her ears just in case.

They ran, shouting, around the corner into Rope-walk Road where ill-kept houses and shops on one side faced the river on the other.

The sun twinkled and glittered in the wake of the barges and tugs as they nosed busily around the big ships. Rip skidded to a halt. 'Look – a timber boat in from Norway!'

Penny fiddled with her safety pin. 'It's not timber, it's made of iron!'

'No, daft!' grinned Rip. 'It's carrying timber!' Owly grinned too and Penny felt foolish.

3

The Dump was round the corner of Ropewalk Road, further along the docks and beyond the waste land that everyone called the Jungle. It drew the children from miles around like a magnet, and was their favourite place to play. It was nothing less than the biggest scrap yard in the world. It was not a pile of old prams and dustbins but half ships, fifty foot long old boilers, old cars and even two rusty army tanks. Penny had heard it said that if you looked hard enough you would probably find Noah's Ark there somewhere. Everything had been there for years and years.

Rip's father, who was a Customs officer, could remember the large hulks of the ships being dragged there during the war. Everything was rust coloured – brown, orange and even red. Sickly, green, spindly trees grew bravely up through car windows and cracks in the old ships. It was possible to wander, crawl or climb in the Dump for hours without being seen. There were times when Rip felt it all looked like a bombed city. Along the rusty buses, up and down crane jibs and through eerie ships' cabins, Owly, Rip and Penny could be lost to the world as long as they chose to be. Many groups of local children played hide and seek in the Dump, hiding especially from Joe Fudge, the night and day watchman who was ever on the prowl. Rip, Penny and Owly had, not only the best, but the most secret hide-out of anybody. It would be impossible for even the most ardent explorer to find their special hide-out without being taken there. Blood-sealed promises to each other ensured its eternal secrecy.

There, in the middle of all the old iron and wrecked cars, completely hidden, was their double-decker bus. All the upstairs seats had been taken out and they had furnished it with old carpets and chairs that had been thrown out from the Wimpy Bar. A TV set that didn't work stood neglected in the corner. A table from a ship's cabin was piled high with all manner of junk that they had 'found' in the Dump. A badly cracked and dented telescope leaned against a silent juke-box.

'Home, sweet home!' grunted Penny puffing up the stairs. High on the ceiling were the words 'The 3 Must-get-nears', which was their own version of the Three Musketeers! Penny and Owly flopped down on an old sofa with no legs and puffs of dust rose in the air. Rip opened the windows on the seaward side.

'Not much movement on the river,' he muttered absentmindedly. 'Must be a strike on or something.'

To all three, this place felt comfortable and safe from all cruel teasing. All three had had more than their fair share of teasing. Every day of her life Penny had heard someone calling her Fatty or worse still Tub Tub. How she hated it and it didn't get easier either. It still hurt even after years of it. Deep inside Penny worried about going up to the 'big school'; they would probably be worse there. It might have been a joke to many children but it certainly wasn't to Penny. Often she cried herself to sleep under the blankets at night.

On the other hand Owly didn't really mind being called Owly, actually he rather liked it. But 'four eyes' made him want to disappear. Owly was saving up for contact lenses but he never got above £3.

Rip, with his delicate chest, was always the last to be chosen when the class at school made two teams. There was only once when he wasn't left until the last, and that was because it was a choice between a girl or him. What made it worse, was the way his mother fussed over him. Winter was terrible when every night he had pepperminty smelling stuff rubbed on his chest. He smelled just like a chemist's shop.

Rip clambered down from the window. 'OK,' he said, 'let's do it then.' Owly and Penny knew exactly what Rip meant. They had done it so often that there was no need for any explanation.

For every time the gang came to their den they prayed. They had worked out for themselves that you didn't have to be in a church to pray. And you could certainly pray without waiting until you had your pyjamas on.

They all sat on the sofa with Penny in the middle.

'One of these days,' sighed Owly, 'God is going to hear us.'

'I think,' whispered Penny, 'God hears all our prayers.'

'Doesn't do much about them, though,' said Rip cynically.

'Tisn't like as if we've got to shout though, is it?' continued Penny. 'God can hear everybody, everywhere.'

'That's like Dad's stereo,' observed Owly. 'You can hear that everywhere!'

They all would have been very embarrassed if anybody in school knew they prayed. This was their special secret and here in the old bus they were very hidden and no one could see them.

Owly picked up a small Bible off the table. It was very old and worn. 'I'll go first,' said Owly.

They each held the Bible in their hands when they said their prayer and when they finished they passed the Bible to the next person. This way, everyone knew when it was their turn.

Owly began to pray.

'Please, God, here we are again and praying very hard.'

He squeezed his eyes together until they hurt.

'Please make me able to see without my glasses – soon! You made people in the Bible who were *blind* able to see, so it's only half a miracle – please!'

He passed the Bible to Rip.

'Oh Great God up high in heaven, lend a listening ear,' Rip prayed with all his strength. 'Please make me grow big and strong like all the other boys in class, so I can be in The Albions football team. And so that my mother will not have to tell everybody I'm delicate and let me go out in the rain!'

Then in turn he passed the Bible ceremoniously to Penny. She drew in her stomach and with real tears in her eyes, she too prayed. 'Please, dear God, let me become thin so that I can wear jeans properly and nice dresses. You know how much I hate, really, really hate everyone laughing at me. And, at the same time, if it's possible for my freckles to go too, I'll be very grateful and never do anything wrong again. But the freckles is second on the list, not the most important thing.'

Then all together they said 'Amen'. They sat quietly for a moment because people always did in church.

Suddenly, there was a sharp clanging, banging noise and Penny jumped. 'What's that?' she squealed.

'There it is again,' said Owly nervously.

'It's getting nearer and nearer.' Rip swallowed noisily.

Straightening up slowly he nervously squinted through a crack in the metal work. 'Oh,' he laughed, 'it's only Joe Fudge!'

'What's he doing making all that noise?' whispered Penny.

'He's banging his wooden leg against everything as he's walking along!' laughed Rip.

If they had only known Joe better! He knew they were there, hiding in the old bus. He had even explored their hide-out when they had gone home! Banging everything with his wooden leg as he hopped along was only his friendly way of warning the children that he was about. He just didn't want to spoil their fun. They ducked down inside the bus and heard the thump, plonk, thump, plonk, fading away in the distance. Joe's wooden leg made round marks in the rusty, dusty path between the metal hulks of long forgotten bumper-cars.

'Wonder what happened to his leg?' thought Rip aloud. But no one answered him. Penny led the other two down the stairs of the bus. Suddenly she stopped on the stairs, crouched low, pointed and whispered. 'Look!' she squeaked. She jabbed the air with her finger, 'Between those two old ambulances.'

Just behind the once white ambulance three men were crouching low, keeping their heads down. Shiftily and silently they stacked boxes and crates.

One man seemed to be on guard. As he leaned on the side of an old crane, his eyes scanned the Dump suspiciously. Then suddenly one of them dragged a large sheet of black plastic over the crates. Owly, Penny and Rip watched, fascinated.

'What are they about, then?' whispered Owly wiping his glasses. 'They look a bit suspicious to me.'

'They're nicking!' exclaimed Rip. His voice had gone as dry as dust. 'They're nicking things!'

4

Early the next Saturday morning the tins clanged on the top of Owly Hooper's washing line. The dreadful clatter woke baby Cyril, Mrs. Hooper and worst of all Mr. Hooper who had been on night shift; but Owly had slept peacefully through it all. It wasn't until 9 o'clock that Owly's slumbers were shattered by baby Cyril screaming when the cat tried to lick the milk off his face. The skull and cross-bones hung sadly in the morning mist. The fog which had hovered stubbornly over the Thames for two days still hung about like a grey blanket. The sea-gulls, fluttering feebly in the wind like dirty pieces of paper, waited for the cooks on the ships to empty their waste bins into the river.

Only Penny had had a leisurely breakfast and that was because Mrs. Bunn, with a horror of seeing Penny fade away to nothing, insisted that she 'topped herself up!' Penny cut her toast into the most ragged soldiers you had ever seen; dipping them into her boiled egg she gave them all bright yellow helmets. Yolk dribbled down the side of the egg-cup and turned the salt hard. 'Watch what you're doing, dear,' smiled Mrs. Bunn. 'That's the best part.' Penny heard nothing as she crunched her toast and thought about rusty ambulances and boxes covered with plastic sheets. They had told no one of what they had seen in the Dump. That was an adventure that they would investigate themselves!

'Adults would ruin the whole thing,' Owly had said, flipping his hair out of his eyes.

The sun had broken through the summer mists and the pavements were steaming when Owly, the last to get there, arrived at Webster's shop. He had walked all the way with one foot on the pavement and the other in the gutter. He had been trying to feel what it would be like to have a wooden leg like Joe Fudge.

'What's wrong with your foot?' inquired Rip swinging on one arm around the lamp post.

'Practising limping, that's all.'

'Oh, I see,' answered Rip, not understanding at all, and added, 'Where you been?'

'Out!'

'What were you doing?'

'Nothing.'

'Who were you with, then?'

'No one.'

'Oh, help,' thought Penny, 'he's in one of his talkative moods.' But Owly really felt this was going to be a good day. His glasses had been newly repaired with a piece of number 8 knitting needle, and six centimetres of what he called 'insulting' tape.

'Well, decided what we're going to do then?' asked Owly tying his shoe laces together so that he would walk in shifting little steps.

'I vote,' said Rip drawing himself up to his full height, 'that we tell my Dad! He's a Customs officer, so he's bound to know what to do.'

Penny gasped and turned sharply to Owly, 'We can't do that! There's no adventure in that!'

'We said we'd investigate it ourselves,' Owly said angrily. 'We got to – so there!'

'Before we do anything,' Penny interrupted, 'my Mum's given me enough money to buy some chocolate – to see me through till dinner time.' The conference suddenly stopped and all three crashed into Webster's doorway. 'Shush!' hissed Penny, 'Mrs. Webster will throw us out!' The shop was as mysterious and dark as a haunted cave. A big black cat flew out of a potato sack, shrieking as if it had been run over by a bus. The children shifted nervously from one foot to the other. Rip coughed loudly to attract Mrs. Webster's attention.

Far away in the back kitchen they could hear Mrs. Webster poking the fire. Someone coughed again, more loudly this time. Nowhere in the whole world was there a smell quite so delicious as the smell in Webster's. It was a succulent mixture of oranges, sweets, bananas, soap, paraffin, bacon, apples, firewood and mothballs. Owly had tried to make a smell just like it at home one day when his mother had gone shopping but it was quite revolting. 'Obviously,' Owly had thought, 'a smell as lovely as that has to have years to mature and grow!'

Penny stubbed her toe on three large cartons by the counter.

'Blummy scum!' exclaimed Penny who had caught the phrase from Owly as easily as measles.

'Shut up, will you,' whispered Owly, angry that there was nothing private with girls about. He promised himself never to say it again and to think up some new words.

Rip stared at the cartons in the half dark. 'Look! Pineapples, prunes, corned beef, cigarettes!' Before he could try to add any explanation Mrs. Webster shuffled, sniffing, into the shop. Penny noticed she had three cardigans on and had mittens on her old hands; which was indeed strange for a summer's day. Apologetically, Penny stuttered, 'I've hit my foot on your boxes – sorry, I won't do it again.' Rip stiffened visibly as something clicked in his mind. Automatically he tried to kick Penny into silence.

'Oh, help!' whined Penny, 'They're attacking me now!'

'Big help, they'll be,' smiled Mrs. Webster nodding at the boxes. 'Just bought them cheap off a very kind man. He said they were discontinued lines or something.' Without moving their heads they all looked knowingly at each other.

'Six strawberry chews, please,' said Penny, pressing her forehead against the wire netting. When she did this it left red square marks on her forehead for ages.

Bursting with questions they all tried to get through the door at the same time.

Outside Owly nudged Rip with his elbow. 'Know what I think?'

'Yeh, I know what you fink and it's the same fing that I fink,' said Penny.

Rip didn't answer. He didn't think – he knew!

Later, alone in the bus, even with such new excitement bubbling up, they first performed their ancient ritual of passing the Bible to each other as they prayed and asked, no, beseeched God to make them like other children – nice and ordinary. Long ago they had realised it was no fun being different. When they had finished they sang together –

      'All things bright and beautiful,
      All creatures great and small,

All things wise and wonderful,
The Lord God made them all,
He made us all so different,
For some are fat or thin,
Our friends are always laughing,
But we must trust in him!'

It wasn't very good poetry but it was the best that they could do.

'I think,' suggested Penny, 'that we ought to start kneeling down like they do in church. Might be better.'

'It doesn't matter,' said Owly putting his glasses in his pocket and squeezing his eyes closed. 'God can hear us standing on our heads!'

'Does that mean' continued Penny, 'that all Australians pray on their heads anyway?' Owly tried to work that one out but it confused him and made his head ache. Anyway he had never seen any pictures of Australians hopping about on their heads.

Rip rubbed the grime off the window with his sleeve. The plastic covered boxes and crates were still there and the three men were nowhere to be seen. 'I bags going to find out,' he said bravely. 'You lot coming?'

'You'll never find your way there,' remarked Owly. 'Not on the ground where you can't see over things! There's too much junk and old cars everywhere; all around it they are! It's okay from upstairs here in the bus – you can see over everything.'

5

The three 'Must-get-nears' crouched on their knees and elbows inside a huge iron pipe. Rusty scales showered down every time they moved or scraped their shoes. Rust got down their backs and into their hair and eyes. Owly sneezed and the sound echoed and thundered down the hollow tunnel. He banged his head on the inside, and down showered a new fall of what looked like brown snow. 'I can't breathe,' Rip complained. 'The rust is up my nose and in my mouth.'

'Only a bit further,' Owly encouraged him, although he was feeling scared himself.

'I'm getting out,' said Penny rubbing blood off her hand. 'My Mum says I suffer from close-to-phobia.' Every word echoed and bounced off the walls of iron.

'Which way now?' enquired Owly blowing the rust dust off his glasses. Then, turning to Rip 'Your hair! It's like covered in brown dandruff – ugh!'

Rip shook his head like a dog coming out of a pond. All around them towered hulks of ships, boilers and old cars. It looked as formidable as a range of brown, misty Himalayan mountains.

'Well, we can't get dirtier – come on.' Penny was off, climbing and pulling herself up as best she could. 'Come on, you boys,' she called over her shoulder. Climbing up was easy for there were many excellent hand and foot holds. Huge bolts and ledges stuck out everywhere. The difficulties arose when they reached the top of the junk and had to balance along narrow metal ridges and rusted through pipes and girders. They all stepped cautiously with arms stuck out at right angles just like tight-rope walkers. Penny stopped dead in her tracks and turned round. 'Oh no, I can't go any further!'

'What's up?' asked Rip. 'It's not been too bad so far.'

Owly indicated with his head, 'That's what's up, that's what!'

Ahead of them, and with no way around, was what looked like a gasworks. A huge iron drum was rusted through. Huge holes, big enough to fall through, peppered the surface, like holes in a giant colander. It would be like walking on thin ice.

'We'll creep around the edge,' said Rip, 'It'll be stronger there.'

With their knees visibly shaking they edged their way around foot by foot, testing each step before putting their whole weight on it. It flashed through Penny's mind that she was the heaviest there!

Gasping and spluttering they threw themselves together in a pile, giggling nervously.

'There, it's all over. Wasn't too bad,' said Rip. Owly and Penny said nothing but breathed deeply, glad it was done.

'Hey look!' Owly pointed down below, 'We're there.'

In their excitement, they forgot all caution and jumped and slid down the junk pile. They didn't even feel the cuts and grazes. But now that they had arrived, they were scared. 'Go on,' Penny said, 'take the plastic sheets off!'

'We'll do it all together,' ordered Rip.

They all gasped at the same time. 'Cor, it's like Aladdin's Cave,' whistled Owly. The pile of boxes stood unveiled. Cartons of tins of pineapple, prunes, corned beef. 'What's Lychees?' asked Penny, trying to read Chinese writing on a tin. She was surprised that there was something edible that she had never heard of!

'Cigarettes, look, there's thousands of them!' exclaimed Owly.

Silently, worriedly they contemplated the boxes. Carefully replacing the plastic sheet Rip said, 'We've got to think, we've got to do something.' They all sat down in the rust.

'We'd better tell my Dad,' said Rip for the fifth time.

'No, I fink we ought to do somefing ourselves and get a reward!' cried Penny.

'What do you think, Owly?' Rip asked.

'I fink, like Penny – get a reward!'

Trudging back through the iron maze, they made their way to their bus. Owly kicked the dust into red clouds. He was thinking. Joe Fudge's hut door flew open with a bang and out stumbled Joe.

' 'ello you lot! Going home early today, aren't you?' The children didn't answer but retreated anxiously. 'What's up, "four eyes"?' He addressed the last remark to Owly – who immediately took off his spectacles and put them in his pocket.

'That's cruel!' exploded Rip, adding as an after-thought 'Peg leg!'

It was so quiet you could hear flakes of rust tinkling as they were blown around inside boilers. 'Sorry, very sorry,' apologised Rip. 'I didn't mean to say that, it sort of slipped out!'

Joe laughed so loudly that the medals on his old army jacket tinkled. He slid his fingers under his cap and scratched his head. Still laughing he spun around on his wooden leg and said 'Come on, come and have some tea with me.' He beckoned them to his hut and added, 'I want to ask you something!'

The inside of Joe's hut was the dirtiest but cosiest place they had ever been in. Old tatty carpets had been nailed to the walls for extra warmth. Chairs, table, cupboards rescued from the scrap yard filled every space, nook and cranny.

'Sit you down,' invited Joe. The three children disappeared into the squashiest sofa they had ever sat on. It was so nice being able to tuck your feet under you without someone shouting at you to take your feet off! In one corner an old oilstove belched blue acrid smoke and since there was no chimney it gathered against the ceiling like a grey cloud. 'Don't worry about it,' said Joe smiling. 'As long as you keep your head down you'll be all right!' The children giggled. 'Go on, you,' said Joe, 'I'll make you the best sandwich in the whole wide world!' Joe stirred corned beef which was spluttering and splashing in the frying pan.

'Lovely smell' drooled Penny, thinking nothing had passed her lips for all of two hours.

'Found it this morning – fell off a lorry!' laughed Joe. 'Really, honest I did. Found it this very morning over by the scrap.'

'I know where . . .' Owly almost blurted it out but was stopped by Rip pressing his shoulder against him.

Joe was so interested in the cooking he didn't seem to have heard. Then out of the blue he said, 'I've heard you lot praying in the middle of the scrap, haven't I?'

Rip looked at his finger nails. He had never felt so embarrassed in all his life. Owly squeezed his eyes together and Penny went bright red. They had been found out and waited for Joe to laugh at them, just like grown-ups do.

Joe scattered a chopped onion into the frying pan. 'Nothing wrong with praying, now – I pray myself – sometimes.' He wasn't laughing, Rip couldn't understand it. Joe added tomato ketchup to what was in the frying pan. 'But I don't pray for my leg to grow,' he chuckled to himself, but looked very serious.

Penny left his remark unchallenged, but asked 'What happened to your leg, Joe?'

Owly sucked in his breath. He had been brought up not to ask embarrassing questions like that. 'The cheek of the girl,' he thought, and muttered self-righteously, 'Don't be rude!'

Old Joe Fudge pushed his cap to the back of his head with the fork he had used to stir the corned beef. 'Many moons ago it happened, me lovelies.' He sang his words out like an old Victorian actor; his arms waved in the air, emphasising each word. 'When I was sailing the Indian Ocean with Abyssinian octopus counters,' he paused and studied the effect his words were having on the children. 'We 'ad to do this job see – we wus ringing octopuses (you know like they ring birds now-a-days) for the King of Balalika!' Wide grins began to lighten up the three faces. Joe continued with gusto, 'We wus paddling in shallow water one day when the mosquitoes were attacking us something ferocious, when along came this 'ere shark, feeling a bit hungry like, and bit it right 'orf!'

Rip looked Joe square in the eyes. 'Did it hurt, Joe?'

'Nah, didn't even notice it till I kneeled down!'

Joe tasted his corned beef fry as if what he had said was an everyday occurrence.

The sofa-embraced audience stifled their giggles.

'Come on' said Joe, 'let me make you a special sandwich.'

Through the open doorway Rip could see two men darting behind an old crashed taxi. Penny, on the other hand, watched Joe, her mouth drooling.

6

Rip grabbed Penny and Owly and dragged them down behind a rusty burnt-out Morris Minor.

'Keep down, you idiots!' he whispered. 'They'll see us.'

The old car gave them as much cover as a dustbin lid in a desert, but the two crouching men, flitting like shadows, gave no sign of seeing them. They vanished behind half a crane leaving the children looking everywhere.

'Now we've lost them. Told you we would,' admonished Rip. He kicked the old car in disgust. 'Come on,' he said, waving his arm. Crouching on all fours, their bottoms in the air like camels, they scuffed and slid along the paths and lanes between the ships' hulks and odd pieces of train boilers and washing machines.

'We can't see where we're going!' whined Owly in a whisper. 'Not crawling along like this anyway.' They were disgusted with themselves and frustrated by what had happened, and sat down, fed up, on the tailboard of a lorry, on the side of which were the words, 'McDonald's Removals – Distance no object'.

'Let's go back to the bus,' suggested Penny. 'At least we'd get a better view from there.'

The boys looked at Penny with their mouths hanging open. Rip patted her on the back. 'Brilliant, Penny, brilliant!'

Back in their double decker bus the three children could clearly see over the tops of all the old wrecks and there, by the old ambulances, the two strangers fumbled and fussed around the bags and boxes.

'We can't watch 'em all day,' said Owly simply. 'We've got to do something!'

'First things first though,' Rip reminded them. They all sat quietly on their chairs and boxes. Penny picked up the Bible and their ritual began again. All their prayers as usual were similar, simple and to the point. Penny prayed that God would make her thin and Owly that his eyes would get straight and he would be able to throw away his spectacles. Rip just prayed that his mother would stop fussing over him, kissing him in front of his friends and thinking he was fragile!

'What are we going to do?' whined Owly exasperatedly. 'You know! About the crooks!'

'I think we ought to tell Joe Fudge, so there!' said Penny.

'Or some grown up anyway!' Rip butted in quickly. 'My Dad's the one, he'll know what to do, him being a Customs officer and all that.'

Owly changed his mind, something that usually happened slowly.

'I think,' he whispered mysteriously, 'we ought to catch them ourselves! And get a reward and our names in the paper, and go to Buckingham Palace and have a medal from the Queen!'

Penny and Rip sat with their mouths sagging open.

'The Three Must-get-nears will do it,' croaked Penny in excitement.

Rip groaned to himself as he thought about all the

trouble that might lie ahead. Inwardly he was cold and frightened but he didn't say a word. After all, they might call him 'chicken'. Suddenly, outside there was an ear-shattering clang and they dashed to the window. The two men were agitated and their eyes darted everywhere. Something had fallen somewhere among the tons of scrap metal but they obviously were suspicious. One man, the taller one with a beard, nudged the other and both dived out of sight. There was no chance of following them, they would never catch them up. The best thing was to leave it for another day.

'Never mind,' said Rip encouragingly, 'we can start painting the inside of our den.'

7

Penny and Rip stood on guard outside the telephone box. Inside, Owly was performing his morning ritual of taking off his spectacles, wrapping them in his handkerchief and hiding them underneath his felt pens in his satchel. No one had any idea that he did this. Owly was ashamed to wear them in school for everyone would laugh at him. All his parents knew was that his school reports were getting worse and worse. They had come to the conclusion that their son and heir wasn't as bright as they had first thought! Actually the explanation was simple – without his spectacles on, Owly couldn't see the blackboard!

Miss Marcham, his teacher, was being driven to the point of resignation for Owly's homework wasn't only good, it was perfect! It made her feel that she was the worst teacher in the world. Rip knocked on the glass window and mouthed, 'Come on, we'll be late for school.' Owly stopped rubbing the red marks his spectacles had made on his nose. They would have gone by the time they arrived at school. Owly had tried playing-up in class so that Miss Marcham would move him to the front desk, 'Where I can keep an eye on you!' He had heard her say that to others. At the front he would have been able to see the board. He had tried fidgeting, copying and even staring out of the window for days. But at the back of the class he stayed 'Because you're too big for a front desk,' Miss Marcham had explained.

In class Owly screwed up his eyes and tried to focus on the board. The long list of words to be included in their own sentences looked like a zebra crossing. Miss Marcham looked up from her desk. 'Who do you think you're making faces at Oliver Hooper?' Owly was so intent on deciphering the hieroglyphics on the board that he didn't hear but continued screwing up his eyes. His face was as wrinkled as a prune!

'Hooper!' yelled Miss Marcham. 'You insolent boy, stop that at once!' The class was in an uproar. Girls giggled and the boys made faces behind their books.

'Sorry, Miss – what did you say, Miss?'

'Don't "sorry Miss" me, Oliver Hooper! You'll stay in after school – half an hour's detention will sort you out.' Miss Marcham slammed her ruler down on her desk. The ruler broke in two pieces and someone giggled loudly but she let it pass.

'Get on with your work, all of you!' she shouted.

Penny carefully wrote the words on the blackboard on a piece of paper. She raised her hand in the air.

'Yes, Penny, what is it?'

'Please, Miss, can I sharpen my pencil?'

'*May* I, Penny, may I, not *can* I! Yes, you may.'

As Penny walked past Owly's desk she slipped the piece of paper on to his desk. 'Thanks,' whispered Owly. 'Contact lenses! That's what I need,' he thought.

Three boys sat in the detention room. Owly for making faces at dear old Miss Marcham, Richard Higgs for sticking a girl's plaits together with chewing gum and Hamid Ashid who had dropped the filling from his tooth down James Cox's ear, because he had called him a crow.

Miss Marcham hadn't heard that bit, of course. James Cox had been taken to hospital in the gym teacher's car. With every bump in the car the tooth filling seemed to roll deeper into James. James, terrified in case it would roll into his heart and kill him, screamed, in turn for his Mother, Father, Granny Parsnip (whoever she was!), his Uncle Terry in Bolton and cousin Helen who was a traffic warden down in Deptford.

Everyone had to sit in detention with folded arms. Hamid Ashid explored the hole in his tooth with the tip of his tongue, and Richard Higgs prepared a fresh supply of 'gumming-up-plaits' material. His jaws never stopped. Owly played 'I Spy' with himself. Mentally he went through the alphabet looking for an object for each letter.

A – Angry teacher
B – Bell jar over broad beans on window sill
C – Cleaners sweeping corridors
D – Dinner ladies, just going home
E – Europe, map of, hanging on wall.

Owly got bored. 'Won't be much longer,' he thought.

Two dustbins, their lids slightly ajar, stood by the bicycle sheds. Out of the dark interiors stared two pairs of eyes! Penny and Rip were waiting for Owly. The moment he came out of school and around the corner, they were going to jump out like demented jack-in-the-boxes, screaming their heads off, and Owly would, they thought, be frightened out of two years' growth! It was boring and cramped inside the dustbins and everything smelled of sour milk. They had to hold the lid ajar with their heads.

'The lid's rubbing a bald patch on my head!' complained Rip.

'Don't worry, I'll knit you a wig like Mrs. Webster's,' giggled Penny. 'Hey, look! Through the gate!' Penny's voice echoed hollowly inside the bin. Rip stared where Penny had directed.

'It's only the lollipop man getting ready to go home!' muttered Rip.

'Hang on,' grumbled Penny, 'I'm stuck and can't move.' Penny promised herself that soon, very soon, she would go on a proper diet.

'Ugh!'

'What's up now?' asked Rip.

'Bar of chocolate got melted in my pocket, that's what! Over there,' added Penny, 'up the side of the Chinese Take-away!'

Rip's eyes followed Penny's directions. Outside the Take-away's side entrance was parked a dark blue van, or what was left of a van.

'So what?' grunted Rip.

'Look what those men are carrying in!'

Penny sounded exasperated by her inability to make Rip see!

Both men, dressed in shabby jeans and navy blue sweaters, worked hard and quickly.

One nervously glanced up and down the alley, while the other nipped smartly back and forth into the side entrance to the shop.

Cardboard boxes marked 'Corned beef', 'Pine-apples' were being rapidly moved into the shop. 'Lychees, look lychees!' Penny almost screamed with excitement. At last it dawned on Rip what Penny was on about.

'You don't think . . .'

'Of course I do!' Penny thumped on the inside of the bin. 'It's them, the men from the Dump!'

All thoughts of giving Owly the screaming abdabs were forgotten. Crouching low behind the school wall, they both spied on the van until the men disappeared inside the shop.

'What can we do?' asked Penny. 'We've got to wait for Owly!'

Rip rolled around and sat down with his back against the wall.

'I don't know, do I – I'm delicate!'

'Delicate my foot!' exploded Penny. 'You're no more delicate than my Aunty Nelly and she's 68 and she was premature too!'

Rip didn't understand but chose to remain silent rather than sound foolish.

'That's it, that's what we'll do!' Without waiting for a reply, Rip crawled on all fours into the bicycle shed. He stared thoughtfully at the tins of paint and brushes and bottles of turpentine left neatly by the decorators.

Penny squeezed around the dustbins after him, clutching the top of her jeans.

'Me safety pin's gone!' she complained. 'Nearly went right frough me and out the other side!'

Ignoring her grumbling, Rip explained, 'That's what we'll do – we'll use a tin of paint!' Penny tossed her head from side to side in confusion. He picked up a tin of white paint and then a piece of rusty wire. Laboriously he punctured a small hole in the base of the tin. Exceedingly slowly the paint started to drip out.

'I'm going across the road to tie this tin under the car. As soon as Owly comes out we'll be able to follow the trail – easy!'

'Oh, watch you don't get caught!' implored Penny.

'What'll they do?' asked Rip. 'Call the police?'

8

Rip, Penny and Owly, their six eyes scanning the road, followed the tiny drips of white paint. 'Don't point at them!' hissed Rip. 'People will wonder what we're doing!' It was obvious where the van had gone faster for the drips were further apart. They did not run but just walked as casually as their excitement allowed. Only their alert eyes could have possibly given them away. Church Street was dingy; once a street where men working in the docks lived, over the years the houses had turned into small shops, cafés and betting shops. Even in summer it was a chilly grey street, but people came from miles around to shop there, for things were cheap and there were often bargains to be snapped up.

Penny was so intent on following the white drips she walked bang into a bus stop and Owly, which was to be expected, didn't see a postman's bicycle by the kerb until he was folded over the crossbar. Half running, half walking, they followed the white dots until they came to Webster's corner, where there was a pool of white paint into which someone had walked, leaving a trail of white footprints going around the corner into Ropewalk Road. Owly looked up. 'Looks as if the van stopped here for a few minutes,' he observed.

From Websters they followed the trail all the way to the Dump. The trail led straight in and ended abruptly as if the van had sprouted wings and taken off across the houses and the docks.

'Vanished, into thin air!' Penny looked underneath an old ice cream cart.

'Can't have vanished,' explained Rip, looking everywhere. 'It's not scientifically possible. The paint probably had all run out, that's all!'

'Don't care if the paint has all run out – look, footprints! The tyres have made footprints!'

Sure enough, the van's tyres had left deep ruts in the rust encrusted soil. Owly put his spectacles back on now that he was off the street. There was no need for him to have done that, for the ruts were so deep even a blind man could have followed the trail.

The trail led frighteningly deep into the Dump, twisting and turning around the old rusty boats and scrap iron. What they were not prepared for, was that they ended up at the tail-board of the 'McDonald's Removals – distance no object' van!

Without any further investigation, they beat a hasty retreat home. They had never in the whole of their lives had more problems, worries or decisions to make. They were quarrelling and niggling each other all the way from the Dump.

'We've got to tell the police!' moaned Penny feeling helpless. 'I'm only a girl and I'm scared, so there.'

'Don't you dare!' chorused Owly and Rip. They had made up their minds that this was something they had to do for themselves.

Penny skipped along the pavement on tip-toe in an effort to dodge the cracks in the paving stones. She was convinced that if she walked on the cracks more than a hundred times, something terrible would happen to her. What, she didn't know, and that, with Penny's vivid imagination was even worse than knowing! The boys bumped the door of Webster's open with their shoulders and slouched miserably inside. They were going to buy one can of Coke and ask, hopefully, for three straws.

'It's sure to happen soon!' fretted Penny. 'I must have walked on miles of pavements!'

Owly and Rip crashed out of the shop, the door bell clanging behind them.

'No Coke,' said Owly simply, breaking open the can of orange.

Aimlessly and unconsciously they wandered around the dull grey streets. Grimy, smashed windows stared out at them like dispossessed eyes. This part of the town always made them wish they lived out in the country somewhere. Without having planned it, they arrived at St. Ann's carved stone archway. The top had been carved into an angel's head; the wings drooping down either side formed the gateway. They sat under the old yew tree in the churchyard and drank their orange, passing it round from one to the other.

'Don't blow – only suck!' said Rip wrinkling his lips.

They were unusually quiet, the graveyard having that effect on them. When there was a conversation it was in whispers. It was the sort of place you went to when you were fed up with the streets or felt unusually sad. You could hardly see the gravestones for long grass, weeds and thistles. Cow parsley grew to over two metres tall. The tombstones, brown with age and soot, looked like mushrooms above the tall grass. Penny stood up, stretched herself, and wandered where no one had walked for years, and read the words on the tombstones. They fascinated her, but always made her sad, especially those who had died as children. When Penny stood still she could hear the darting and scampering of small animals. She had only seen mice and voles but there were hedgehogs and moles. Miss Marcham had said that there were badgers too, but no one had seen one. Brambles, like spiky octopuses, had grown around and over marble angels and stone urns.

No one had worshipped in St. Ann's for years. On the door in the west wall, a sign read 'Beware of falling masonry'. It was altogether a very sad place to be in on a lovely sunny day. She reached out and almost touched a red admiral butterfly before it flew away. Owly and Rip ambled over and sat on a tombstone.

'Here'ya, Penny, finish it off!' They handed her the remains of the orange. Penny sighed and leaned on the grave.

'Thanks' she muttered and sucked the can dry with one long gurgle and splutter.

Owly looked up and squinted through his glasses. 'We'll have to set a trap for them, that's what!'

'Set a trap for what – voles, moles, poles or what?' grumbled Penny.

'You know, those crooks in the Dump!'

'Oh them . . .' she started to say something else but instead she screamed and jumped up clutching her hand.

'What's up now?' Rip joined in but there was little real concern in his voice. 'Calm down sissy!' He took Penny's hand, and there on the loose skin between her finger and thumb, hanging by his pincers was an insect. It was bright orange in colour with a tail that could bend over like a scorpion. He knocked it off on to the ground.

'Coo – it's a bloodsucker!'

'A what?' cried Penny trying to get the whole of her hand into her mouth and sucking it madly.

'A bloodsucker!' repeated Rip with relish.

Penny's world suddenly went dark.

'You'll die, you know!' said Owly uncertainly, 'if you cut yourself between your finger and thumb – then you'll die.'

'Will I, will I really?'

'Or get lock-jaw' said Rip with a glimmer of hope. 'And that's just as bad in the end 'cos you'll die from starvation – slowly!'

Rip looked around at the graves and jokingly added, 'I wouldn't go home if I were you! Just hang about a bit!'

9

That night Penny went to bed early to die!

Although it was the middle of summer and during the day the tar on the road had melted and stuck to their shoes, she still took a hot water bottle with her. She also took a bag of crisps, half a packet of biscuits and a jam and banana sandwich – there was nothing like dying in comfort. If her fingers were going to swell up and in turn change from red to purple and then drop off, there was no need to diet any longer.

'You all right, dear?' Mrs. Bunn called anxiously from the bottom of the stairs . . . she had wondered what on earth Penny was doing going to bed this early but didn't ask any questions.

'Don't forget to say your prayers, dear!'

'No, Mum!'

Penny prayed for the whole family and all her friends in turn. She prayed for the whole world and that there would be no wars in their street; and then, that she'd get better from the bloodsucker's bite.

'Oh God – please make me better. If you do I promise I'll be very good from now on; and I'll go to the Family Service without grumbling. I promise I'll give half my sweets to the poor and love all little children – even Owly's Cyril who spoils everything.' She stopped praying; the bite was getting redder all the time. Penny's mother would wisely have said, 'Of course it's more red – stop sucking it, daft!'

'The poison's made my feet hot now and it's going all through me!' thought Penny forgetting all about the hot water bottle. She thought about the tombstones at St. Ann's and made up an inscription for her own tomb!

'Here lies the body of Penny Bunn,
She was fat but lots of fun!
Now in heaven she's gathered in,
Happy at last because she's thin!'

That night she thought seriously about God and heaven and Jesus. She felt very comfortable knowing that he was her friend. Penny wondered why her mother and father never went to church with her? It made her very sad thinking about it. 'It's only boring sometimes' she thought.

Even Penny knew that in heaven everything was perfect. There was no pain there and everybody was made perfect, just like Jesus. Blind people would be able to see and people with one leg, like Joe Fudge, would have two legs. Everyone, the Bible said, 'would have a new body'. Penny wasn't quite sure if she'd like *everything* new. She was very familiar with the body she had; all she wanted was the old one slimmed down a bit! But she would be happy to leave it to God.

The next morning Penny had porridge, bacon, egg and sausage, toast and marmalade for breakfast. She had just realised she hadn't died during the night! She couldn't possibly have sausages in heaven; it would be more likely to be milk and honey!

10

'It's great living by the river,' said Rip. 'It gives a new dimension to life!' Owly and Penny spun round from hanging over the rail of the ferry boat. They were on the river steamer going from Greenwich on a trip up the Thames. They pulled faces at each other. 'A new *what* to life?' they said together.

'Dimension!' Rip answered earnestly.

'What's a dimension?' asked Owly, amazed that a little delicate chap like Rip could even say such big words, let alone know what they mean.

'It means, like an extra bit that you didn't have before!'

'Why didn't you say that in the first place?' grunted Owly, throwing the last of his crisps to the sea-gulls.

'Dimension, dimension, dimension!' repeated Penny to herself, so that the next time she heard the word she would recognise it and say 'Hello!'

'Are those crooks in the Dump a new dimension then?' Owly enquired.

'Yeh, suppose they are really,' answered Rip.

The boat was packed with holiday-makers, going for an outing on the river. It was the first week of the summer holidays and school was forgotten.

A grey gull that looked as if it could do with a spin in Owly's mother's new, super automatic washing machine, perched on one leg on the ship's rail.

'Look – he's only got one leg – just like Joe!' observed Penny.

'Nah, the other one's just tucked up in its feathers,' explained Owly. They all stared, trying to make sure. If the gull had two legs it certainly wasn't going to give them the satisfaction of knowing.

Usually in the winter you could rake the rubbish and old tin cans off the surface of the river, but today it was as clear and blue as the sky. The reflection of the sun on the water made their eyes water and they turned sharply and faced the stern of the boat. There, sitting on wooden benches was a crowd of old ladies and gentlemen from St. Barnabas's Evergreen Club for Old Age Pensioners who were singing, laughing and clapping their hands. It wasn't long before they started dancing! Penny, Owly and Rip started to smile and then laugh out loud, but not rudely. You could see the old ladies' bloomers – they were all pink. 'They must only make pink ones!' thought Penny, slightly non-plussed.

'Poor old Joe Fudge couldn't dance like that' said Rip feeling sad, 'with his great handicap.'

'Handicap! Shouldn't you say leggycap?' asked Owly in all seriousness.

Owly automatically thought about his spectacles and bad eyesight, Penny's roundness and Rip's delicate constitution.

'We'd just about make one good person out of the three of us,' he sighed. Then to everyone he said, 'God isn't answering our prayers, is he?' No one had an answer to this thoughtful question.

The old people had stopped dancing. Little old men with no teeth and bent old ladies with walking sticks, two grandfathers with deaf-aids and one in a wheelchair were all singing at the top of their croaky voices,

'If I were a butterfly,
I'd thank you, Lord, for giving me wings,
And if I were a robin in a tree,
I'd thank you, Lord, that I could sing,
And if I were a fish in the sea,
I'd wiggle my tail and I'd giggle with glee,
But I just thank you, Father, for making me "me".'

By the end of the trip they had explored every inch of the boat. They had been up and down every stairway three or four times, waved to the Captain, seen a lady's hat blown over the side and had slipped where someone had been sick!

At tea-time the boat berthed back at Greenwich but no one could get off the boat because of the old man in the wheelchair! He was making everyone laugh so much that they couldn't push the thing straight! It kept getting wedged and stuck in the gangway.

'Beep, beep, brum, brum, out of the way,' he shouted, 'or I'll wallop you with my teddy bear!'

A little, round old lady in a blue coat and white hat with cherries on it, had to sit down on a wooden slatted bench. She laughed until tears ran down her face. She was clutching her handbag to her stomach.

'Ooo, ooo, ooo – dear me!' she squeaked.

'Aren't they happy?' remarked Penny. A sense of shame began to embarrass the children. They had so much and yet grumbled to God continually.

11

'He's been kidnapped – they've got him!' Owly spun around like a top, his eyes darting everywhere. The children scuttled and nosed around Joe Fudge's hut in the Dump. They couldn't see Joe anywhere!

'No message, no footprints, no blood!' said Penny slapping her thighs in exasperation. His hut was as empty and ghostly as the Marie Celeste. On his oil stove another corned beef dinner bubbled and spluttered. The smell was wonderful. Penny licked her lips appreciatively.

'Can't have gone long,' said Rip with the air of a detective. 'We've got to see him!'

Then they all joined in shouting 'Joe! Joe! Where are you Joe?'

Penny, always resourceful, stirred the corned beef and took it off the stove. She surmised that the burnt circles on the top of the old TV set were where Joe put saucepans, and set the frying pan on a burnt mark.

'We'll hang about a bit and wait,' volunteered Rip. 'He'll not be long with that stuff still cooking!'

The boys sunk into the springless sofa. There was something special about Joe's hut. Rip preferred it to his own sitting room, which smelled of polish, where the sofa was new and hard and where you couldn't put your feet on anything without putting newspaper there first.

Suddenly the door burst open, as if it had been hit by an elephant in a hurry, and in blew Joe like a summer gale.

'Ta-ra! ta-ra!' he sang out. He waved two more tins of corned beef in the air. 'They're growing on trees now!'

'Joe, where've you been? We didn't hear you coming!' complained Penny, digging her hands into her hips.

Joe hiccuped a laugh. 'Look, look, look!' he pointed excitedly to his wooden leg. 'On the end! Great, isn't it?' Joe had fixed a wheel castor off an old chair on to the end of his pegleg!

'But you can't stand still on a wheel!' said Owly.

'I've got one good leg, haven't I?' Joe countered.

He emptied the contents of the frying pan on to a plate which had 'Sunny Blackpool' printed around its edge, and gently lowered himself down on to a sack filled with straw. The smell was a glorious mixture of hundreds of chip shops, Chinese take-aways, and Sunday lunches all rolled into one! They suddenly all felt exceedingly hungry. Penny swallowed hard and tried to stop a rumbling down below! Joe pointed with his fork to his newly equipped wooden leg. 'Do you think,' he asked through a mouthful of crispy corned beef, 'that I could get a job with the Council with that thing? I could do them white lines down the middle of the roads.'

Before they could reply, Joe added, 'You lot hungry then? I could make you a fried corned beef sandwich.'

'You can't have fried corned beef in a sandwich!' squealed Rip indignantly.

'What! You can have anything you like in a sandwich! You can have chips or ice cream or brussel sprouts or cold porridge! Anything, just anything you fancy!'

Rip thought of his fussy mother and his eyes grew wider and wider. Penny licked her lips and smiled pathetically, 'I'd love one, Joe – please!' she croaked.

'That's my girl! You're a girl after me own heart!'

Joe made each of them a sandwich. Fried corned beef, tomato ketchup and two pickled onions – whole – which made a rather lumpy sandwich!

Joe pressed the slices of bread together very hard to stop anything falling out. Owly fidgeted and stared at the two lumps the onions made. 'What's them, Joe?'

'It's called a camel sandwich, me lovelies! Go on, get your insides wrapped round it!'

'My mother would have a fit,' thought Rip. 'Me, delicate and eating pickled onions!'

Penny made a mental note to ask Joe for the exact recipe.

Penny secretly nudged Owly, grinned a tomato ketchup smile and said, 'Joe – please, how did you lose your leg?'

Joe seemed confused, 'Haven't I told you afore?' Three heads shook negatively. 'Well then, t'was like this, see. Oh, t'was nothing very exciting, but when I was your size – no, smallerer than you, my Mum put my pyjamas in the washing machine a bit quick like!'

'Well there's nothing wrong with that?' questioned Penny, nearly suffocating with laughter.

'None, my dear – but I was in 'em see!'

This time the three burst out laughing and corned beef splattered everywhere. To add colour to his story Joe added, 'The water went 'orribly red!'

The corners of Joe's mouth crinkled into a smile. No one questioned the truth of Joe's story. They all knew that it would be different next time anyway!

Rip coughed nervously, 'Joe, we've really come to tell you our secret and ask you for advice.' Joe polished his plate with a piece of bread to save washing it and licked his lips.

'Off you go then – get it off your chest!'

Rip told Joe the whole story from beginning to end. The food dump in the middle of the scrap yard, Webster's cheap bargains, the Chinese Take-away, the tin of white paint and the McDonald's removal van. When it was all over and deadly silent, Joe breathed deeply and stared at the children strangely as if not knowing quite what to say to them. 'I've been finding tins of corned beef too! You know about that!'

Penny edged forward in excitement. Joe wrinkled his forehead. 'There's a lot you don't know about and understand,' he continued. Rip's head, buzzing with all sorts of ideas, lolled to one side like the head of a rag doll.

Then Joe said something very strange and mysterious.

'For goodness sake, don't tell anyone! You'll spoil everything!'

The children gasped and stood up.

'What shall we do then, Joe?' asked Owly who had been silent for a long time.

'First – will you do as you're told?' whispered Joe.

The children nodded like model dogs on car back windows.

Without any more questions or strange looks Joe said, 'Tell the police, that's what! But don't do anything yourselves!' As they rushed out of the door Joe called after them, 'And remember, don't tell anyone else – not a living soul!'

But they were gone.

12

Rip perched, or rather clung on to the window sill of his bedroom. Realising that if he fell backwards he would probably break his neck, he hung more tightly to the edge of the open window.

'What on earth is he doing?' he muttered to himself, squinting through the opening. 'He's gone potty!'

At the far end of the garden Rip's father was digging a hole! All you could see were shovelfuls of earth flying into the air. There was nothing new about Mr. Potts digging in his garden, for it was his favourite hobby, but he was behaving in a most odd and mysterious manner.

'Why' thought Rip, 'is he trying to hide it?'

Rip's father had casually built a screen with his old wheelbarrow, peat sacks, bits of wood and old bean poles; anything he could lay his hands on!

It was behind this screen that Rip's father dug secretly and mysteriously.

'Something's up!' exclaimed Rip. 'Something's definitely up!'

It had slipped Rip's notice that Dad had occasion-ally glanced up at his bedroom window and had grinned slyly!

Mr. Potts made a big show of sticking his spade into the bank of dry earth and without raising his head, peered through his eyelashes up at Rip's window.

Smiling knowingly, he made his way up the garden path towards the kitchen.

'It's his cup-of-tea time" said Rip to no one but himself. 'Something big is up and they're not telling me!'

As soon as he heard the kitchen door slam, he jumped off the window sill and crept silently down the thickly carpeted stairs. In his socks he made less sound than the cat.

From his precarious position, hanging over the landing banisters, he could see and just about hear his parents talking. He made a mental note that they were having chocolate biscuits too! But there was something unusual about their voices and he just couldn't put his finger on it. He had never heard them speak so oddly before!

'I've found it, my dear!' said Mr. Potts excitedly and fell into his chair. 'After all these weeks of digging, I've found it!'

Mrs. Potts hesitated as if not knowing quite what to say.

'I'm delighted for you, dear,' she said and added almost too excitedly, 'you'll be in all the papers!'

Mr. Potts grimaced as if someone had scratched a fork along a plate! He shook his head slightly, signalling that perhaps she had gone too far.

'The lost Roman City of Thames!' grinned Mr. Potts. 'After all these years of secret searching and studying in the library archives! We've found it at the bottom of our own garden!'

Rip's mother clapped her hands together excitedly.

'Do you think there'll be a reward, dear?'

Again Mr. Potts waved down her enthusiasm.

Rip ran on tiptoe back to his bedroom and threw himself backwards on to his bed.

'The rotters – they're keeping it all to themselves! Why didn't they tell me? Don't they trust me or something?' His head buzzed with all the newly discovered possibilities. What would Penny and Owly say, for nothing like this had ever happened before! *His* father discovering an ancient, ruined city. They'd certainly have him out in front at school to tell everyone. That would be great! He began to think about all the money they could make by charging people who would come to see the mosaic floors, marble statues and pillars! There may even be a burial chamber like King Tutankhamun! They were going to be famous and have their pictures in all the papers!

Gloom settled over Rip, like a black cloud.

'But why haven't they told *me*?' he complained bitterly. His thoughts were startled by his mother's shrill voice, from the bottom of the stairs.

'Robin, dear?'

'Yes, Mum?' he shouted inquiringly.

'Won't be long. Your dad and I are going to the garden centre.'

'OK!' answered Rip. They were going out and now he would have the opportunity of exploring the hole properly.

'I've not finished my model of London Bridge yet!'

'There's a good boy. Keep your window closed and all the cold air out!'

'Oh, heck!' thought Rip, 'Will they ever stop? I'm all right!'

The front door slammed with a bang as Rip checked from his window that they really were going.

Before they had reached the lamp post at the end of the street he was downstairs pulling on his trainers.

Rip stared disappointedly into the mysterious hole.

'There's nothing there – sweet nothing!' he grumbled. 'Just a dirty big hole!'

Nevertheless he jumped down into it. As he landed loose earth scattered everywhere. Idly muttering to himself he kicked odd clumps of soil. It was a good thing that Penny and Owly were not there. They would have laughed themselves silly at his foolishness. Rip stared into the corner of the hole. He could hardly believe his eyes and slowly a smile began to crease his face. Protruding from the crumbling soil was an ancient stone slab.

Forgetting that he was wearing his best jeans, he fell on his knees and scratched away like a puppy unearthing a long lost bone. Quickly, more of the stone slab appeared.

Rip stopped and took a deep breath for there in stone, chipped out clearly by a Roman stone mason hundreds of years ago, was the letter 'Y'.

As soon as he recovered from the initial surprise, he began feverishly scratching again – working backwards a letter 'T' was added to the 'Y'. Rip laughed out loud as an 'I' came into sight and then a 'C'. He stood up brushing his knees as he unbent – there it was 'CITY' as clear as the day it was carved. His finger-nails were so packed with earth that they hurt, but he threw himself into the digging and scraping with energy that he never knew he had.

More and more letters appeared. With a low, sad moan Rip threw himself backwards against the earth wall of the hole. Soil cascaded down the side, filling his collar.

'Oh, no!' he yelled, flinging his head with a jerk towards the clear blue sky.

The truth on the stone slab mocked him silently as the word 'ELECTRICITY' blazed unkindly as if inviting the world to witness his stupidity.

From the kitchen door-way burst waves of uncontrollable laughter.

'Ever been had?' cried Mr. Potts. 'The joke's on you!'

Rip froze, he could not believe his ears! They had set him up, and, he thought, in the most cruel way. How could they be so unkind and thoughtless?

They had arranged the whole thing!

Try as he might, Rip couldn't see the funny side. This wasn't a joke at all! It had made him look silly and stupid. He blushed to the roots of his hair and with tears burning in his eyes, scrambled out of the hole that had suddenly become so uninteresting.

Mr. and Mrs. Potts stood on the kitchen step not knowing quite what to do. They had stopped laughing and were shuffling awkwardly.

Mr. Potts coughed nervously.

'All right, son? It's only a joke!'

And trying to justify their actions added, 'You ought to be able to take a joke at your age!'

Rip's eyes blazed with anger.

'I'm going to see Owly,' he shouted in return.

'But wait a moment – let me explain!'

Rip kicked the earth around the hole in his temper.

'I'm sorry – but I'm going to see Owly!' he yelled again. 'Expect me when you see me!'

Mrs. Potts squeezed Mr. Potts' arm.

'Oh dear, what have we done?'

'I think we've gone too far, dear – better go in and make a cup of tea. I don't think he'll be very long.'

Rip's feet flew, hardly touching the ground, down King Edward's Road. He wasn't running anywhere in particular – just getting as far as possible from home, that hole and his parents!

'They've never loved me,' he muttered to himself through his tears.

'They only say they do because they've got me. Wouldn't be surprised if I was adopted anyway!'

It never crossed his mind that he had played tricks on others, tricks that were just as bad.

He didn't remember the time when he placed an over-ripe tomato on a chair just before Penny sat down! Or the time when he stuffed matchsticks down the drinking fountain at school just before Benny Hogg went for a drink. A mouthful of matchsticks had shot into Benny's mouth giving him the surprise of his life and putting him off drinking fountains for ever. But that was all right! The houses and shops in King Edward's Road flashed by in a hazy blur. Blinded by his anger, Rip noticed little of the peeling paint and broken windows.

On and on flew Rip.

He didn't even see 'Maison Fred' the ladies' hairdressers.

Normally he would have stopped and pulled faces at the young men who were having their hair done in a *ladies'* hairdressers! Turning off King Edward's Road, by the Curry House, he crashed down into the cutting and towards the docks. It wasn't as if he was intentionally making his way there, but rather that he seemed drawn by some invisible force towards the water.

'R-i-p!' Penny and Owly shrieked together.

They had just ambled into King Edward's Road and had seen Rip careering down the hill like a car out of control. But their shout was drowned by a hooter blast from a ship in the docks.

'Come on!' cried Owly. 'After him!'

Because Rip had had too much of a start on them and Penny wasn't in any way as fleet footed as a gazelle, Rip had vanished by the time they had reached the entrance to the cutting.

'Now we've lost him!' puffed Penny, hitching up her jeans.

'No – just mislaid him, that's all!' answered Owly.

'Do you think he's just hiding at the bottom?' remarked Penny by way of a suggestion.

When they reached the wharf they both scanned the quay with their eyes.

'He's disappeared!' said Penny, nonplussed.

'Can't have vanished into thin air. Can he?'

Owly jumped up on to a crate for a better view, but still couldn't see Rip anywhere. There was a strange stillness along the dock side. A black and white cat slunk more deeply into the shadows out of the hot sun. The sea was as still as a sheet of steel. The only movement was alongside a ship called 'Southern Star' from Panama. Some men were slowly shifting and loading sacks on to a platform that was in turn hooked on to a crane.

'He was running so fast,' said Penny, 'perhaps he couldn't stop and ran straight into the sea!'

Owly sighed with impatience at her stupidity but she had only tried to make a joke.

'Girls!' he muttered to himself.

'Well, he could, couldn't he?' exploded Penny indignantly.

Owly said nothing but continued to shuffle along the quay wall.

'Let's have a look – he's probably just run on to the old pier.'

Owly turned round and faced Penny. By way of an apology he muttered, 'You are coming, aren't you?'

But Penny understood that he was really saying, 'Do come, Penny – I'm scared to go on my own!'

13

As Rip had hurtled down the steep cutting he realised
he was running too fast to stop, so he took the corner
in a wide, circular turn and slowly came to a halt. He
breathed deeply to get his breath back and sat on a
capstan. Absentmindedly he kicked stones into the
sea.

'They were rotten to do that to me!' he thought to
himself. 'Fancy going to all that trouble, just to trick
me and have a laugh.'

He stooped down to pick up a stone and immediately stiffened. His eye was caught by movement on
board the ship. Two workmen were busily winding
and stacking huge ropes. Rip watched out of interest.
Slowly it began to dawn on him, and he could hardly
believe his own eyes – it was them! The two men from
the Dump!

'They are the ones who have been stealing all those
tins and things!' gasped Rip to himself.

Immediately forgetting about 'Electricity' he rolled
off the capstan into a hiding position behind some
foul-smelling sacks. He could see everything but they
couldn't see him. Looking over his shoulder to make
sure that no one could see him from behind he
groaned and gasped, 'Oh no! They'll spoil everything!'

Owly and Penny came tearing out of the cutting
with as much noise as the circus coming to town. Since

he couldn't shout without being spotted, he made himself as small as he could and squeezed into a gap between the sacks and crates.

'Go away!' he willed Penny and Owly in vain. 'Oh, please go away – you'll ruin everything.'

Owly and Penny ambled over to the water's edge, looking everywhere.

'Oh no!' said Rip again, 'They'll be seen!'

'Psst – hist!'

'What's that?' Penny jumped.

'What's what?' asked Owly.

'That hissing noise.'

'Steam or something from the ships.'

'No, listen!'

'There's nothing.'

'There it is again – you're not trying!'

'Psst – you two – idiots!' hissed Rip.

Penny turned towards the sacks and saw Rip crouching there. How she didn't scream 'Rip' remains a mystery.

'He wants to play Sardines!' she thought to herself. Rip was holding his finger to his lips and with his other hand was urgently signalling them to get down.

'What?'

'Get down!' mouthed Rip. It was difficult making himself understood without actually shouting and it would have been exceedingly dangerous to stand up. Although they had no idea what was the matter, Owly and Penny fell flat on to the wooden planking of the wharf. Through the cracks Penny could see the grey-green water swirling and ebbing around the seaweed covered bollards. She turned her head towards Owly.

'He's gone potty!'

Owly hooked his glasses back over his ears, 'Not half as potty as some people I know!' he grinned. With his right hand Rip signalled them to keep down and crawl over to where he was hiding.

As she wriggled along the wharf like a bulky, overfed snake, Penny caught her safety pins between the planks and they dug deeply and painfully into her.

'Ouch!' she whined, but bravely kept on crawling.

They shuffled up into a sitting position next to Rip, behind the sacks.

'What 'ya doing?' Owly inquired, pushing his glasses back along his nose.

'Why didn't you stop when we called you?' complained Penny.

'We nearly shouted our heads off!'

'Listen!' explained Rip, ignoring their questions. 'They're down there on the deck of the ship – those two from the Dump!'

'What!' exploded Owly picking up his glasses that had jumped off his nose.

'The two crooks?' piped Penny shrilly.

'Yes, the two crooks! You bananas or something?' Penny sulked.

'What *are* we going to do?' asked Owly in amazement.

'There's only two things we can do. We can either go home or spy on them!'

'We can go to the police?' suggested Owly feeling frightened.

'Oh spy, spy!' Penny spluttered. 'Let's spy on them!'

'That's what I thought,' said Rip.

They turned over on their stomachs and edged up towards the top of the sacks.

'There they are!' said Rip nodding with his head.

The two men, quite oblivious to three pairs of watching eyes, continued winding and tying ropes. Without any doubt, they were the same men with the same sad faces and shifty eyes.

'Let's get closer,' Owly suggested, rubbing his eyes behind his glasses.

Crawling along the wharf on their elbows and knees was painful. Wood splinters embedded themselves in their knees, but they certainly got a better view from behind the gangplank. Suddenly, everything on deck changed quickly. The men glanced quickly and furtively over their shoulders and then darted towards some bulky tarpaulin that seemed to have been thrown casually up against the wheel-house. One of the men flipped it up and the other began dragging small boxes from underneath.

'They're at it again!' said Owly, focusing his glasses on the end of his nose, turning them into binoculars.

The boxes were quickly stuffed into a large canvas bag to which a long rope was fastened.

As soon as the bag was full, it was thrown over the seaward side of the ship and the rope tied to the handrail. It all looked perfectly organised and efficiently planned.

'Penny!' ordered Rip, 'you slip away and get the police.'

'Me? You go! I'm not going by myself!'

'Oh, Penny!'

'I'm too scared to go by myself. Anyway the police wouldn't believe me.'

'Go and tell Joe Fudge then! He'll go to the police for us!'

'Look!' Penny commanded, pointing towards the men.

Another man had appeared at a door, wiping his hands on a filthy white apron, and made eating gestures with his hands before disappearing back into the darkness.

Penny recognised 'eating' signs with little trouble!

'It's their dinner time,' she whispered wistfully to the boys. 'They're going down below to eat.'

'I think you're right, Penny,' said Rip trying to stretch his aching limbs without standing up.

The silence that followed was no reflection on the turmoil that was in their minds.

Everyone was so busy thinking, they didn't think of talking!

'Are you thinking what I'm thinking?' said Owly turning and smiling at Penny.

'I'm thinking,' said Penny squeezing her stomach, 'that it's dinner time and back in our house my Mum is cooking chips and fishfingers and apple crumble . . .'

'Well, you're not then!' said Owly disgustedly.

He changed his direction of conversation.

'You, Rip?'

'What now?'

'I think we boys ought to nip down on to that ship and collect that bag of stuff as evidence and then take it to the police station!'

'I was thinking something like that too,'

They turned to Penny who was feeling ashamed that her longing for food even dismissed important things from her mind. Before the boys could say another word she pleaded, 'If you're going – I'm going too!'

'But Penny – you can't run fast!' Rip grumbled.

'I'll keep watch then!'

The boys whispered together secretly.

'All right then! But you must obey orders!' admonished Rip.

Penny smiled happily, knowing she had won.

Since the men had indeed gone down below, there was no further need to crawl secretly.

They sauntered along the harbour wall as bold as if their parents owned the docks. Rip was even brave enough to whistle.

Getting on board was going to be another matter! But one which easily solved itself when all the workmen stopped work and ambled off in different directions to have their lunch.

They lost no time at all and without any fuss or panic walked up the gangplank with as much confidence as if they were going on a world cruise!

'Owly!' whispered Rip.

'You go to the hatchway and keep your eyes open in case they come back.'

'You, Penny . . .'

Penny cut him short with a wave and flutter of her arms.

'I know, I know. I'll get the knots undone and get the bag of stuff!'

'No, no Penny, wait!'

'It's all right, don't fuss. I'm good with knots!'

Penny was already at the rail, tugging and pulling at the knots in the rope that held the sack.

'It's coming – won't be long!'

'Penny, wait,' called Rip anxiously. 'The sack is heavy, it'll . . .' The words of warning arrived too late.

Penny uttered a muffled shriek and clasped her hands to her face.

Rip and Owly ran to the side of the ship just in time to see the sack plummeting down into the grey sea.

'Oh! I'm sorry!' Penny apologised. 'I only pulled one end of the rope and the whole thing came loose.'

'All our evidence gone!' sighed Rip.

'I said I was sorry – please don't be angry.'

The boys looked at Penny, sighed, but said nothing.

'Let's go home,' said Owly. 'It's our dinner time too.'

Walking down Ropewalk Road, Rip kicked an ice cream carton into the gutter. He sniffed and said, 'Hands up all those who say we go to the police tomorrow.'

Three hands slowly and sadly crept up into the air.

'All right – see you in the Dump tomorrow.'

14

Rip paused at the gap in the hedge that led from the roadway into his back garden. It was only on his arrival home that he remembered the morning's tragic events. The hole was still there, silently mocking him. Dad was running up and down the lawn behind his mower. The events of the morning cascaded through Rip's mind and he started to smile.

'CITY, indeed,' he muttered.

Mr. Potts noticed Rip as he turned the mower and immediately stopped the engine and wiped his hands on the seat of his trousers.

'Everything all right then?'

He wasn't sure which was the best way to start talking. Should he apologise to Rip, or give him a gentle row for charging off and behaving in such a childish way? Anyway, he obviously thought that Rip had had enough hassle for one day and tested the atmosphere with, 'What do you think of our lost City, then?'

Rip raised his eyes to meet his father's.

'Gave me a bit of a shock!' he grinned. 'Get it? Electricity – bit of a shock?'

Mr. Potts groaned, comforted.

'Lunch is nearly ready – better go and get washed.'

Very little was actually said as they ate their lunch. His parents thought he was quiet because of what had happened. But Rip had said little for his mind was on other things. The events at the docks and the Dump had become frightfully important. Although he knew that they ought to go to the police, he still had visions of becoming a hero and proving how strong he really was.

'Great,' he muttered to himself without realising.

Later, he sat for a full five minutes holding a piece of plastic London Bridge in his hand with glue running down his fingers. Unseeing, he stared out of his bedroom window. The whine of the vacuum cleaner droned on downstairs unceasingly.

Rip jumped, startled by his mother's voice, calling, 'Owly's just phoned dear – about going to the Dump. But I told him you had been out long enough today and all the fresh air had gone to your chest.'

'Oh, Mum, everything's all right – honest.'

'I know what's best for you, son. I know you'd go out and struggle on bravely.'

'Oh crumbs,' Rip hissed, 'mothers!'

But if the truth had been told, they had all had enough excitement for one day.

When Owly had returned home, he had been shouted at for forgetting to take baby Cyril with him as he'd promised. The baby had been left in the full sun in the garden and had turned bright pink. Not only that, but a seagull had gone and given him a third, strange looking eye right in the middle of his forehead. There was no more 'out' for Owly that day. He spent the rest of the time doing running repairs on his glasses and thinking about how he could make enough money to buy contact lenses.

Penny had been greeted with, 'Penny, love, you look half starved – just you sit yourself down and we'll top you up in no time.'

Penny's mother wasn't the best cook in the world but what she lacked in expertise she made up for in bulk and enthusiasm. Penny's plate had been stacked so high she couldn't move it without sending peas ricocheting all over the table. Every time a fork was dug in, fish fingers cascaded around the plate in a golden fringe. Penny had to refuse a third helping of apple crumble.

'You poor thing, love,' sighed her mother. 'You sickening for something, then?'

Penny's famous safety pin went ping!

15

The Three Must-get-nears would not have known what to think if they could have seen Joe Fudge. He crashed out of his hut like a whirlwind.

'I'll have to hurry,' he grunted to himself. 'Before everything is blown!'

Gone was his clownish smile. In its place was a worried, anxious frown.

'We'll have to move quickly before the plan's ruined!'

As he hurried along the rust strewn paths in the Dump even his unusual walk seemed aggressive and urgent. Gone was the sloppy, waltzing gait. Now it was militaryish and official. Joe swung through the galvanised sheet gate of the Dump and hopped, skipped and jumped along the mean little street. The junk of the Dump, spilling outside, had gathered around wheelless cars and old washing machines that people had left in the street when they found the Dump closed. At the corner of Railway Terrace he slipped into Eddie's newspaper shop and bought a newspaper. But it was small change he really wanted and not the paper.

Outside the shop he glanced furtively up and down the street and in one swift movement darted into the telephone box. Another quick glance over his shoulder and then he was talking seriously and urgently on the phone. The door flew open with a crash and Joe was half way back to the Dump before the door fully closed. With lightning speed he flew into his hut and emerged with a broom and made his way to the other side of the children's hide-out. Of all the strangest, silliest things to do, Joe began sweeping the earth and rust paths in between all the piles of scrap iron. It was as silly a thing to do as hoovering a wood or scrubbing a motorway! It looked as if Joe was not only missing a leg but a few nuts and bolts too! Joe flung his broom to one side and hurried as quickly as he was able towards the thieves' hidden hide-out. With amazing agility for a man with a wooden leg, he climbed over the mountain of junk that completely hid the secret horde. The climb down was even harder, for Joe had to select carefully each stepping place for his wooden leg. The going was easier on the flat ground as he shuffled across the bulky tarpaulin.

Lifting it up, he stuck his hand deeply underneath, smiled to himself because everything still felt all right and then hurried away back to his hut to wait.

16

There was not a cloud in the sky as Owly, Rip and Penny scuffed along the wharf wall. Even the sea was bright blue. 'The police won't believe us you know!' grunted Penny for the tenth time. 'They never believe kids.'

Even optimistic Rip was inclined to agree. 'They think all kids do is pinch things and bend car aerials!'

Penny started to walk, carefully missing all the cracks in the planks.

'I saw a dead cat this morning,' said Owly thoughtfully. 'That means I'm going to have bad luck all day. Unless I see another one, that is!'

'That's daft!' laughed Rip. 'There's no such thing as luck – good or bad. I walked under four ladders one day and nothing happened. Glad those men are not here today,' he continued, sitting down on the edge of the quay and dangling his legs over the edge. The other two joined him.

'Know what?' said Owly.

'No, what?' answered Penny sucking her cheeks in so as to make her face look thin.

'We haven't prayed for a long time about our problems'.

'I have – every night,' said Rip proudly. 'But nothing ever really happens.'

'Don't think God has time for little things,' said

Penny wistfully. 'He's only got time for famines and earthquakes and harvest festivals and . . .' Penny suddenly stopped, pointed into the sea below their feet and gasped. 'Look!' she laughed, stabbing her finger to where the sea was swirling around the bottoms of the bollards. 'The sack! The sack of stuff we dropped in the sea!'

'*You* dropped, you mean!' said Rip.

'I'll get it,' volunteered Penny. 'Since I dropped it in – I'll get it!'

'Watch yourself, Penny,' warned Owly.

But Penny was, of course, already clambering half-way down among the beams and joists like a rotund monkey.

'It's easy!' called Penny. 'There's more cross-beams than a ladder!'

She swung with her left hand and tried to grab a post with her right. Her hold was not firm enough and in an effort to stabilise herself with her feet, she lowered her weight on to a beam covered with slippery seaweed. Her feet flew from under her and over she went head over heels into the sea!

'Oh, Penny!' laughed the boys.

Penny squirted water like a whale.

''S all right!' she spluttered. 'I can swim!'

Penny climbed back up and stood, feet apart, on the wharf, sea water slowly dripping off her, forming puddles around her feet. 'Can't go home all wet. I'll be murdered! I'll have to dry off first.'

'It's a good thing it's so sunny.' Rip tried to be encouraging. 'Come on, may as well go to the Dump. The sack has vanished!'

Owly and Rip led the way up the cutting towards

King Edward's Road. Penny squelched behind, leaving a long wet trail like a happy slug.

*   *   *

They sat in their bus hide-out feeling miserable. 'Thought we were going to catch them ourselves,' said Owly polishing his specs. 'Now we've got to go to the police!' No one moved, the silence and feeling of defeat was depressing and demoralising. That is, until Penny jumped up, hoisted up her wet jeans and yelled, 'We can *still* do it ourselves – NOW! and we've got to do it before we go home. I've got a plan.'

Owly and Rip looked at Penny suspiciously.

'Listen!' continued Penny, turning from the window, 'they're out there now, aren't they?' The other two nodded. 'Well, what we'll do is, that one of us crawls over to where they are and shouts at them, then they'll chase us and we can run and lead them back to the bus!'

'What will we do with them, then?' said Rip, thinking the whole plan was ridiculous. Penny swallowed hard, flapped her arms excitely and added, 'We'll run straight *into* the bus and as soon as they're inside, one of us who will hide underneath the bus will dash out and slam the door and lock it! You can, there's a bar thing.'

Penny was out of breath in the excitement of explaining her idea. 'Then the other one of us will run for the police because they will be safely locked up in our bus! They'll never get out because all the windows are stuck or rusted and there's rubbish piled against the rest!'

Owly smiled indulgently.

'Know what you've forgotten, friend?'

'No, what?'

'What about the one that leads them into the bus? They'd be locked in with them!'

This time it was Penny's turn to smile.

'Forgot to tell you,' she gasped, 'the one who leads them, charges straight into the bus and out through the front exit!'

'Brilliant!' grinned Rip wishing he'd thought of it. 'We'll have two doors to lock! But we'll do it!'

Plans were made and jobs allocated and material to wedge up against the two doors placed conveniently but inconspicuously ready. They worked like beavers. Owly was elected to run for the police – since he was fastest. Rip was going to entice them away and lead them into the bus, which was rapidly being turned into a prison. Penny was going to squeeze underneath the bus and slam the door when everyone had run in. The plan seemed perfect and nothing could go wrong! They went over the details again and again and again. They even had two rehearsals.

'Right, let's go then!' commanded Rip. 'Everybody to their places.' An uncertainty crept into their hearts.

'Do you think it's really all right?' asked Penny nervously.

'Of course it's all right,' Owly assured her. 'It's got to work! To your stations everyone!'

Owly hid in the old crane from where he would have a good view of the bus and be able to see when the doors had been locked. Penny sucked in her stomach and rolled under the bus. Rust and dust got up her nose but she didn't sneeze. Rip picked his way carefully through the scrap iron and rusted junk in the direction where he knew the men were hiding.

He turned, and although he could see no one, he waved bravely but didn't feel so brave. As he crept stealthily and quietly he thought of everything that could go wrong. Penny could get stuck under the bus and not get out in time to lock the door! Owly could fall or smash his glasses and get caught before reaching the police! From where he crouched behind what was left of an old fish and chip cooking range Rip could see two men covering the boxes with plastic sheeting. 'Here goes!' Rip said to himself. He jumped up on an old oil drum, cupped his hands around his mouth and shouted, 'Hey, you!' His voice trembled a little but carried clearly in the evening stillness. The two men jumped up, startled. Their eyes darted everywhere. Fearing being caught they charged erratically everywhere – trying to hide, like ants exposed to sudden sunlight.

Rip continued shouting. 'My mother wants to know if you have any free corned beef or lychees!' The men spotted him and the battle was on. Both men shouted something and started to scramble and claw their way across the scrap iron towards Rip. Rip laughed and did a little dance 'Yoo-oo!' The men didn't waste any time but continued clambering, slipping and running towards Rip. What an obstacle course the Dump could be!

Rip waited until it was nearly dangerous. He could see the snarling mouths of the two men. Then as soon as he could hear what they were saying to each other, he was off. He made sure not to run too fast so that the men could always see him. As he turned to see how far they were behind him he slipped, his leg going down between two steel funnels. He felt the warm stickiness of the blood running down his leg and soaking his sock. Fear now took away pain. He was so scared he would have run even with a broken leg! Rip was easily the fastest when climbing over the old ships and boilers. He could jump about like a mountain goat. He worried about the last, flat run to the bus; in the open it would be a different matter! He jumped down from an old bulldozer, waited until the men came into view again and then ran straight along the path between the wrecks. Rip swung around the pole on the platform of the bus and charged upstairs, only just in time to hear them scampering up the stairs after him.

As soon as he saw their heads appearing at the top of the stairs he was out through the emergency exit slamming the door after him. As he rolled old oil drums over the exit he could hear the men shouting the horrible things they were going to do to him. Penny rolled out from under the bus as soon as she heard the footsteps on the stairs inside and crashed the door closed. She tried to lever the railway sleeper on to the door but it wouldn't budge! 'Owly, quick, quick, please help!' Owly scrambled and slipped down from the crane and ran over just as Rip joined them. Together they managed to heave the sleeper towards the door until it fell 'crash' into place.

'We've done it! We've done it!' yelled Penny.

The men were running around inside banging at all the windows and shouting the most horrible things.

They looked terribly ferocious Rip thought, and they reminded Penny of gorillas in cages in zoos throwing themselves against the bars. They could not make out what they were shouting but the bus shook vigorously from side to side.

'I'm off for the police' shouted Owly. It was out of fear that Penny added, 'We'll come with you too!' The bus wavered as the men, realising that they had been trapped, rushed around in panic banging and screaming.

17

'What can we do for you, young lady?' the police officer leaned across the counter in Bank Street Police Station. 'Lost your dog, have you?'

'No, sir,' Rip butted in.

'Lost your way then?'

'No, sir,' continued Rip shaking his head. 'We know where there's some crooks, that's all!'

'Oh, aye,' said the sergeant, straightening up. 'Someone pinched your ice lolly, then?'

'No, seriously, sir,' interrupted Penny. 'We know where there's a pile of stolen food, tins of lychees and corned beef and cigarettes and things.'

The officer's attitude changed immediately. 'Hang about,' he said cautiously. Then turning to a hatch in the wall behind, he called through. 'I think you ought to come out here, sir.' Then he stuck his head right through and continued in a whisper. What he said couldn't be heard.

To the right of the duty officer a glass door opened and a policeman beckoned with his finger, 'In here then and tell us what's happening. Sit you down and I'll go and get the inspector.'

The three children were left alone.

'There's no bars anywhere, observed Owly, and added after looking around, 'Where do you think they keep their guns?' The door opened suddenly.

'This is Inspector Thompson, children.' They all stood up.

'Sit down, it's all right. Now, let's start at the beginning, not all at once – you tell me!' he pointed at Owly. Ten minutes and a lot of scribbling later, everything they knew had been written down in a notebook with a spiral top.

'I think,' said the inspector, 'you had better come with us and show us exactly where everything is.'

Rip's eyes lit up. A ride in a police car was a dream. It wasn't even a Panda car, but a big, shining white one with a light on top. Owly smiled to himself as he sat next to a policeman in the back seat and hoped that some of his friends would see him and think he was a criminal being taken off to jail! But he was disappointed that they didn't switch on the flashing blue light! The police car shrieked to a stop, sending showers of rusty dust into the air. Penny was the first out, 'Over here, sir – they're over here!' The three policemen were followed by another with a dog and Owly and Rip.

'There had better be something here,' growled the inspector. The door of the bus lay wide open and the railway sleeper had fallen to one side. The bus was empty! Rip groaned, 'Oh no, not again!'

'Now then, you lot,' said the sergeant, 'you know what happens to those who give false alarms, don't you?

'But they were here – honest, sir' pleaded Owly.

The sergeant had begun to take his notebook out of his pocket when Joe Fudge came hopping and wheeling around the side of the bus. 'Can I help you, gents?' he said doing a spin on his wooden leg. The police tried not to smile.

'Who are you then?' asked the inspector suspiciously.

Before Joe could answer, the sergeant leaned forward and whispered something into the inspector's ear. The inspector's eyes twinkled knowingly. He shrugged his shoulders and said, 'You may as well – the cat is out of the bag now!'

The sergeant turned to the children and with a great sigh said, 'You lot have nearly spoiled everything. Joe here is our lookout man! He's been watching those men for ages!'

'Oh, no!' groaned Owly.

'Oh, yes!' said Joe bowing theatrically. 'Joe Fudge, Guardian of this noble pile of junk. Late of Her Majesty's navy. Maker of fried corned beef sandwiches extraordinaire!'

By now, the police were actually laughing.

Then Penny slapped her hands over her eyes. 'Idiots!' she gasped. The laughing stopped abruptly.

'Who do you think you're talking to?' spluttered the inspector angrily.

'No, no, no – not you, sir, US! We can still show you where the stolen stuff is – then you'll believe us!'

'We do believe you,' smiled the sergeant, 'and we also know where the stuff is! We just told you – Joe has been watching them for us for ages but couldn't tell you!'

'Oh!' said Penny feeling rather deflated.

'Never mind,' he added, 'Go on, lead the way.'

They took the officers to where the food was hidden. Owly noticed that the police couldn't climb over the scrap very well.

'There it is!' Rip pointed to the clearing in the middle of the scrap and as he did he slowly lowered his arm. There appeared a croaking in his voice, 'It's gone! It's all gone! They must have moved it all!'

Joe butted in, 'It's all right, sir, I bugged the stuff!'

Penny was horror-struck. 'Honestly officer, it was there!'

The policemen looked at each other.

'The van, there's the van too!' Rip reminded everyone.

They all stood quietly by the rental van as Joe let the tail board down. 'Empty – nuffing 'ere at all!' he wheezed.

The inspector turned to the children, 'Now then, do you know anything about this?'

'Oh,' exclaimed Penny, 'It's their van, cross my heart and hope to die.'

'No, not dying – but prison perhaps,' the inspector snapped, jokingly.

'Oh heck,' groaned Owly as he sat down on the tail board. Shamefully he looked at his shoes – and there, still bright and glistening were drips of white paint. 'Here's a clue for you!' Owly pointed at the white dots.

'Leave everything to us and don't mess in police work!' commanded the inspector. 'You've been watching too many cops and crooks on the telly. Just go home and forget everything. We know what's happening. See, Joe here is *our* man and *he's* keeping watch for us!'

18

The summer was the hottest for years. Gardens cracked, water was in short supply in some parts and the sea-gulls had flown far out to sea. Children were playing in the street in swimsuits. Old men sat on walls and front door steps all along Ropewalk Road. Trees thought it was autumn and turned their leaves brown. Grass, that grew in abundance between cracks in the pavements and gutters shrivelled up and vanished. Penny and Owly in swimsuits and Rip in jeans (because he had skinny white legs) pressed their noses against Webster's shop window. The yellow plastic bananas were now much longer and very much thinner.

'Don't think she will,' grumbled Rip.

'We'll try anyway. No 'arm in asking, is there?' said Penny hopefully. The bell clanged piercingly as they opened the door. 'Shop!' shouted Penny.

Far back in the shop she could hear Mrs. Webster muttering, 'Coming! Coming! Nobody's got any patience these days.' She appeared in the doorway behind the counter.

'Oh, it's you again,' Mrs. Webster scratched her ear with a pencil.

Without thinking Owly said, 'My Mum says you shouldn't put anything in your ear smaller than a football!' He blushed when he realised what he had said.

'What was that?' Mrs. Webster asked as she looked at him over the top of her glasses.

Penny quickly came to the rescue, 'Is it possible to buy just one pound of those potatoes, please? That's all the money we've got enough for.'

Mrs. Webster made some grunting noises that sounded like 'not worth it really, all my time and bother,' but at the same time she weighed out a pound of potatoes for Penny, who was glad to notice that the scales read 1¼lbs!

'Thanks, Mrs. Webster, thanks very much.'

Feeling they owed her an explanation, Penny continued, 'We're going to light a fire in the Jungle and cook our own dinner. We're going to boil the potatoes in a tin and cook Owly's sausages on sticks.'

'Be careful to put the fire out after you've finished!' Mrs. Webster warned.

She put three iced buns on the counter. 'There you are – there's your pudding for you!'

The children were speechless. 'Cor! Thanks, Mrs. Webster – you're a good 'un I tell you.' Mrs. Webster mumbled something about being young herself once.

The patch of ground known locally as the Jungle was a plot of land cleared by bulldozers but never built upon. The years had rolled by until today you could get lost there! Grass, weeds, bushes and brambles all struggled to dominate. Most probably it was called the Jungle because years ago one of the ships had dumped a load of rotten dates there, and some of the date stones had grown into straggly date palms. They bore no dates, however, in this cold climate but as trees they just managed to survive. It had been known for TV programme producers to descend on the

Jungle to film stories of Africa and India. Today, it was full of children too warm to run around; most were lying in the sun getting browner every day.

Owly, Rip and Penny had found a dip in the ground where they could be alone. They had no problem in lighting their fire. The problem was keeping it burning. The very dry wood burnt too quickly. It turned to ashes in seconds. 'We're not going to have enough wood to boil the spuds!' Owly commented. 'There's none around anywhere.' Too many children had lit fires in the past.

'You know what?' said Rip. 'I'll go back to Webster's and ask if she's got any spare wooden boxes.' Without waiting for an answer Rip got up and charged through the nettles. He didn't have to worry about scratches or stings with jeans on. Penny and Owly lay back on the grassy bank. Above, the sky was cloudless. Palm leaves raggedly framed patches of bright blue sky. It really felt like Africa.

Rip closed Webster's door with his left hand. In his other hand he held an orange crate. In one movement he swung around and tossed the crate on to his shoulder. His blood ran cold. Icy fingers crawled up his spine; and for the first time in his life, his knees honestly and truly knocked together.

He could hardly believe his eyes!

A man was standing glowering and forbiddingly blocking his way. 'Your Ma still want a tin of corned beef?'

Rip hurled the orange crate into the man's face and using the lamp post as a pivot, spun around in the opposite direction and ran off as fast as a greyhound after a rabbit. The corned beef man clutched his bleeding nose but did not chase after Rip, instead he waved with his spare hand in the direction of the parking lot. The same old tatty van that the children had seen before jerked and spluttered into the open and pulled up outside Webster's. He opened the door and jumped in. 'He's round the corner,' he growled to the driver. 'Come on, get a move on!'

By now his features were indistinguishable, there was blood everywhere. 'Go on – after him,' he spluttered through bloody lips. 'He'll get away!'

A police car nosed suspiciously around the corner by the butcher's shop. 'Hang on, hold it – it's the Old Bill!'

The corned beef man crouched low in the van, so his bloodied face was hidden. They wanted to avoid the police like the plague. Police Constable Morris chattered aimlessly with his driver, 'Nothing happening today, mate – drive over to the Rec and let's watch the kids playing football!'

'Nah,' suggested the driver, 'better if we went back and warned those kids in the Jungle about their fires.'

'Ah – go on, don't spoil their fun, you were a kid yourself once!'

'But the place could go up in smoke y'know!'

'They can't do much damage, it wouldn't be the first time the fire engine's galloped around there.' The police car slowed down and the driver nodded towards the old van outside Webster's.

'Wonder if that old crock has passed its M.O.T. Looks only fit for the scrap yard.'

P.C. Morris laughed, 'What a pile of junk, it's only held together by string!'

'Come on, over we go!'

The radio crackled and spluttered to life, 'Car no. 127 proceed in a westerly direction along London Road. Robbery at Laundromat at junction of Albany Road and Queen's Dock approach.' The police driver revved up and glanced across to the van, 'Your lucky day, mate' he said to himself and then added, 'Look out villains, the sheriff's coming!'

The two men in the van sighed with relief. 'That was a close one!'

The driver grunted, 'We'll get 'orf then – after that perishing kid! Otherwise the Old Bill will be after us!'

Rip's lungs were at bursting point as he tore along Ropewalk Road not looking to the right or the left, and certainly not looking behind him and losing valuable time. His blood pounded in his head. His legs, like pistons, thumped up and down almost mechanically.

The fear that gripped his throat could only be compared with the tight agony in his heart. 'The Jungle. The Jungle' he whimpered to himself, 'I must get to the Jungle and the others.'

In spite of his cold, clammy fear, the thumping in his heart and the agony in his legs, Rip felt flushed with pride. 'Look at me, I'm running and running nearly a hundred miles an hour! And I'm delicate and catch colds and can't eat pickled onions!' He jumped and easily cleared the ditch, two metres wide, that separated the Jungle from the road. He landed perfectly on his two feet but as he threw himself forward he twisted his knee mercilessly. The searing pain shot like hot knives into his thigh and his face twisted in agony. As he rolled over and over in the nettles the pain vocalised into shrieks, 'Owly, Owly – over here, Owly!'

'Hark!' mimicked Penny blowing into the fire. 'Someone calleth!'

'Calleth be blowed,' admonished Owly. 'It's Rip and he's in trouble.'

Owly and Penny kangarooed through the Jungle calling as they jumped nettle patches and rusty beds, 'Rip – where are you?'

'Here, by the ditch!' The voice sounded frightened and in pain. When Owly and Penny cascaded down in a storm of dust and leaves beside Rip, he was rolling around in a pitiful state.

'What's up, Rip – what's happened?'

'Stop 'aving us on!'

'It's me leg – I've bust it or something; but it's the men in the van, they're after me; they saw me outside Webster's,' he gasped, and gripped his knee. 'Oh! – I can't get up! Don't touch it!' He slapped Penny's thoughtful hand away. Owly put his hand under Rip's arm, 'Come on, we'll help you.'

'No, you idiot! I can't run and they're bound to see us.'

Penny stood up and peered over the top of the nettles and tall grass. She immediately threw herself back down on to the ground. 'They're there – by the Dock gates,' she squealed.

Bob and his mate clambered out of the van and half closed their eyes as they searched the area. 'They must be around here somewhere!' hissed Bob. 'Hang about and listen.'

'We're done for – we've 'ad it!' whined Rip between clenched teeth.

Penny began to suck her thumb – something she always did in moments of crisis or extreme hunger. 'I knew something terrible would happen.'

90

Cautiously Owly raised his head. The corned beef man was coming across the edge of the Jungle.

'He's coming,' whispered Owly watching carefully.

Bob stood on the edge of the dry grass of the Jungle, 'I bet the varmints are in there somewhere!'

Casually he lit a cigarette and then holding the burning match, stared at the growing flame. He hastily dropped it as it burnt his fingers, and an evil smile curled up his lips.

Owly rolled over onto his back. 'He's going to burn us out – I know it! I know it!'

'He can't, he can't, Rip can't move – he'll be done!' cried Penny.

Owly, ever resourceful and brave, took command.

'There's only one thing for it, Penny and me will run for it and draw them away from Rip. He'll be all right for a bit!'

'Don't leave me!' cried Rip fearfully.

'You'll be okay, we'll come back for you.'

Rip could see that this was the only sensible thing to do.

'I can't run,' complained Penny worriedly.

'I'll hold your hand and drag you along,' Owly ordered. Penny smiled, pleased to think of her hand being held by Owly.

'Don't be long,' pleaded Rip holding his knee.

Without any more fuss or planning, Owly grabbed Penny's hand.

'Right – as soon as I say "go" – run and don't think, and as you run, shout like mad!'

Penny sniffed hard, 'OK then!'

As the corned beef man opened the box of matches Owly yelled, 'Geronimo!' and he and Penny were off, running and jumping through the grass like a bad TV commercial for springtime.

'There they go!' The corned beef man dropped the matches and ran towards the slugging van. 'Cut ahead of those kids!'

Soon clear of the Jungle, Owly and Penny ran like lightning along the old harbour wall. 'Run, keep on running,' yelled Owly.

The road was empty – everyone was having lunch somewhere. The danger they were in could not be shared by anyone. The van, although ancient, was gaining on them.

'Help! Police!' shouted Penny.

The road remained silently empty.

Never had they run so hard before.

As they turned the corner into Copperworks Road, Owly saw the old, rusting railway lines leading to the Docks. 'Run in between the lines,' he shouted, 'the van can't follow us there, it's too bumpy!'

'My strap's gone!' shouted Penny clutching the top of her swimsuit, and with that, she stumbled over the railway line, fell flat on her back and rolled into the road. Owly was after her like a brave knight on horseback. 'Up, quick!' he said, lifting her on to her feet.

Before she could properly stand up the van screeched round the corner. Owly only just had time to see the look of terror and horror in the eyes of the driver as he heard the scream of poor brakes trying vainly to bring the van to a halt.

The van slewed sideways, turned over and hit them both!

19

Penny sat up in bed. She tried to move and make herself more comfortable, but her plastered arm made it impossible. Once again she stiffly turned her head to the left.

'You sleeping, Owly?'

Owly said nothing. He looked a bit like an Egyptian mummy with his head all bandaged up. He put down his comic. 'Rip's coming to see us in five minutes,' he muttered cheerfully. 'That'll be nice.'

All the other children in the ward held Owly and Penny in great esteem. They were heroes! They had actually been responsible for catching two crooks!

The comments had come quickly and ungrudgingly. 'You'll have a medal,' said one boy.

'You'll go to see the Queen and be touched with her sword,' said the boy who was having an operation for sticking-out ears.

The girl who had worn away half her finger in the school's electric pencil sharpener had suggested that they might even get a reward. Although they were sore and stiff Owly and Penny basked in their pleasant admiration.

The glass door at the end of the ward clattered open and an army of parents, grand-parents and friends spilled into the disinfected room.

The room was filled with 'Darlings!' 'Yoo-oos' and

'Here we ares' as people waving comics and clutching parcels made their way to various beds.

'Hi!' greeted Rip as he hobbled to the edge of Penny's bed.

'You're not allowed to sit on the beds!' warned Penny.

Rip presented Penny with a bunch of roses from his garden.

'They're lovely,' said Penny.

Rip waited a while before bringing out, from behind his back, a box of chocolates and a bunch of grapes. On seeing Penny's eyes light up, he quickly added '*Between* you!'

Rip described for the fourth time how the van had turned over and had trapped the two villains until someone had phoned the police and an ambulance had come.

Everything had ended very quietly really, but they were certainly in for a reward. There was even a photograph of the crash in the 'Evening Echo' and there under the picture were their names!

'How are you two feeling?'

Doctor Tyndale had slipped silently up behind Rip. He didn't wait for a reply. Tapping his clip board on the edge of the bed he continued, 'You are both very fortunate children! It's strange really – you,' he said pointing at Penny, 'can thank God you are nice and plump! Because you are so well upholstered you just bounced when the car hit you! And as for you Tutankhamun,' he smiled towards Owly, 'you can also thank the good Lord who looks after you that you were wearing spectacles. If it hadn't been for the protection of those specs the shattering glass of the windscreen would have gone in your eyes and you would certainly have been blinded!'

Those were words that Owly and Penny would never forget.

'There's someone else outside to see you,' said Rip, and edged towards the ward door. He swung the door wide open and on his one wheel in glided Joe Fudge with his arms outstretched like wings.

All the children in the ward cheered, and Joe blushed!

'Joe! How'd you do that?' laughed Penny. 'That's brilliant!'

'I learnt myself,' grinned Joe, revealing his missing front teeth! 'I think I'll become a ballet dancer when I grow up!'

Everyone giggled.

Secretly, from under his old coat Joe sneaked out a parcel covered with newspaper, and slipped it under Penny's pillow. 'Don't open it until it's dark and everybody's sleeping,' he grinned.

That night when everyone was fast asleep Penny opened her parcel and whispered across to Owly, 'Owly – toasted corned beef sandwiches – want one?'

Rip, Penny and Owly made a promise that from that day to this, every night when they said their prayers they would thank God for *not* answering their prayers.

Penny thanked God that she was nice and round. Owly thanked God for his specs, and Rip thanked God that he wasn't delicate at all. He just had a mother who was a bit, sort of careful!

But best of all they thanked God for being so great, and that he knew what was best for everybody and could see the end from the beginning!